Table of Contents

Prologue: Shared Pain

I woke up in the castle storeroom.

It was musty. I really hated it in there, but I felt pretty well rested.

Snoring . . .

I could hear rhythmic snoring coming from the pile of straw next to me. A young girl named Raphtalia was sleeping there.

Let's take a minute to review what's happened.

My name is Naofumi Iwatani. I'm a sophomore in college.

I was born in Japan, just like everyone else. To be honest, I was always a bit of an *Otaku*.

I was at the library flipping through a book called *The Records of the Four Holy Weapons* when, for whatever reason, I found myself transported to the fantasy world it spoke of. I had been summoned to serve the role of the Shield Hero.

The world was suffering under "waves of destruction," in which hordes of monsters and horrible disasters spilled over from other dimensions through rifts in space. Four heroes were summoned to protect the world from harm. I had a shield on my arm that I couldn't remove—maybe it was under some sort of curse? I found myself unable to go on the offense at all. All I could do was defend.

But I had some experience with online MMORPGs, so I focused on defending myself and recruited someone else to attack for me.

We set out on our adventure, and I was very excited. But I fell into a wicked trap. Someone framed me for a crime I didn't commit, and I found myself convicted. So nobody trusted me from that point on. I couldn't make any friends or get anyone to help me, and they ran me out of the castle without a word. I was in a really tough spot.

I figured I would just not do anything. I thought I didn't have to fight against the waves of destruction. I was wrong.

The waves of destruction arrived around once every month, and we heroes were instantly transported to the site of destruction.

I was forced to protect a bunch of people that I didn't care a lick for—it wasn't fair at all. I did all I could to raise money to survive, and all the while people jeered at me. They threw rocks at me.

So that girl that was sleeping next to me, Raphtalia, she's a demi-human slave. I bought her.

Slavery still exists in this world, and in this particular country, Melromarc, there were people with animal attributes called demi-humans. They were sold into slavery all the time.

When I bought her, she was just a little girl, but as we leveled up she grew very quickly, until she appeared only slightly younger than me. Apparently demi-humans grew differently than the rest of us—they developed based on their level, not their age.

In the beginning, I thought I'd work her hard, considering she was a slave and all. But soon enough this pompous jerk named Motoyasu forced me to battle. During the fight, Raphtalia believed in me and attempted to sacrifice her own freedom to protect me. Well, there were other things too, but in the end we became close friends, and we trust each other deeply.

Honestly, for the longest time, I couldn't have cared less if everyone in the world just dropped dead. But now, I sort of feel like I want to help out.

"Ah . . ."

Raphtalia woke up and rubbed her eyes.

"Good morning, Mr. Naofumi . . ."

"Ah . . . Um . . . Morning."

Looking at her again, I thought she really was quite beautiful.

Her face was like a work of art. I could use words besides "beautiful," but I'll hold off for now.

Her hair was brown and hung in loose curls down her back. Her eyes were big and bright. They were the color of a deep red tea. They were the most beautiful eyes I'd ever seen.

With all that she had been through, I don't know how her eyes were still so pure and kind. They were too pure to belong in a body of her age. They really were the most charming thing about her.

I leveled up and earned money with Raphtalia until the first wave of destruction came. It was the first wave I'd seen, but it was the second wave that had visited the world. It was a hard fight, but I'll tell you all about that later on. The really tough stuff happened afterward.

"Should we go get some breakfast?"

"Yeah. Think we can get some in the castle dining hall?"

"Perhaps . . . Let's go see."

So we made for the dining hall, and I kept running over all we'd been through.

By the way, my bad name had yet to be cleared. The castle officials treated me coldly. Anytime I tried to go to the cafeteria the guards would turn me away. The knights and other heroes are still eating, they'd say. Come back when everyone else is done. If I hadn't been forced to be the Shield Hero, if only I could have attacked, I'd have taken care of that whole crowd a long time ago.

And I wouldn't have let being a "hero" stop me!

We finished eating and were led into the audience chambers.

The occasion was to be one of celebration. We were all about to be compensated for our efforts during the wave of destruction.

Give me a break! If they were going to make us wait a day before they paid us, they should have said so in the first place! I swear, Trash was just trying to piss me off.

The thought of spending another second with this group of jerks was unbearable. What if I got an ulcer?

The person I called "Trash" was, in fact, the king of this land, Aultcray Melromarc . . . the Second? The Third? I can't remember. Anyway, apparently he was the one who summoned me here.

When I'd been framed and accused and convicted, he never even tried to find out the truth. He just let it all go and let me take the fall. Some king, right? And then, just last night, he used his authority to throw a fit and cause a big disturbance.

"Now then, we will distribute the reward funds for your performance in the last battle and also your preparatory funds for the next wave."

That's what I really needed: money for preparations.

Trash had promised to give the money to all of us heroes.

An attendant entered the room. He held a bag of money stiffly in his fist.

"Now then, to each of the heroes."

I turned to look at the bags of money.

At the very least, they were sure to provide us with 500 pieces of silver for each month.

What would I buy with it?

It would probably be wise to start with a new weapon for Raphtalia.

Or maybe it was time to invest in some better armor. Come to think of it, I also wanted some new materials to use for making medicine. I could let my shield absorb them too. I could see what kind of abilities they got me. I listened to all the coins sliding around inside the bag and fantasized about what I would buy.

The attendant held the bag open so that I could see the contents.

I quickly counted the coins inside. Yes, there seemed to be 500 pieces in there.

"To Mr. Motoyasu, both in recognition of his performance and to express our future expectations for him, we present 4,000 silver."

Hey now!

I was taken aback. I staggered and quickly looked over at the very heavy bag that Motoyasu was now holding. If I were to say something, it certainly wouldn't get me anything but contempt though, so I just bit my tongue. I felt my fingers curling, involuntarily, into a fist.

They called this guy Mr. Motoyasu, but his real name was Motoyasu Kitamura. Like myself, he had been summoned from an alternate Japan, and he was one the four heroes—the Spear Hero.

He was 21 years old. The other heroes apparently had experience in, and knew all about, this world. They knew it from some game they had played back in their own worlds. But they didn't share any of that knowledge with me. They framed me and kicked me when I was down.

So this Motoyasu guy apparently ended up getting stabbed because of his womanizing and then woke up here. That's just what he says though, so who knows if it is true or not.

He only allowed women into his party. It was like he was setting up some kind of harem or something.

Last night, thinking that I was abusing Raphtalia as a slave, and to satisfy some kind of messiah complex, he decided to try and "save" her from me and challenged me to a duel.

Normally a duel would have to be agreed on by both parties, and both parties would need to have something to gain by it, but not this one. He forced me to fight when I had nothing to gain. Obviously I refused, but Trash stepped in and forced me to participate. If I lost, they would take Raphtalia from me, and if I won, I got nothing—pretty damn unfair, if you ask me.

Anyway, I had to fight him, and I didn't want to go down without a fight. So I did what I could with what I had and ended up pinning him. It looked like I was going to win, but then someone cheated and attacked me from behind to ensure I lost.

In the end though, Raphtalia refused Motoyasu and came to my side on her own, and that was that.

So basically this guy is the cause of all my troubles.

Honestly, he looks like your typical ladies' man. He's handsome enough and entertains himself by hitting on girls all the time.

He wore a glamorous, polished silver breastplate. He was very clearly on the winning team.

"Next, Mr. Ren. In recognition of your fulfillment of our request, and of course to express our trust and hopes in you, your reward is 3,800 pieces of silver."

Him too?!

Ren was standing there pretending to be unfazed, but he was obviously jealous of Motoyasu's more impressive funding. He let the bag of silver hang heavy from his hand. I could hear him muttering to himself, "Just 'cause you're the king's little favorite . . ."

Ren's real name was Ren Amaki, and just like me, he had been summoned here from another Japan somewhere. He was the Sword Hero. I think he said that he was 16 years old.

Yes, he was from Japan too, but not the same Japan that I was from. In his world they had something called VRMMO, and it was some kind of system that let you enter a virtual world completely. Wherever that Japan was, it was more technologically advanced than the world I was from.

Apparently there were many different Japans. Had you asked me a year ago, I probably would have jumped at the chance to visit his world.

He was about as tall as you would expect a 16-year-old to be, and his face was a pretty little thing. A very princely swordsman, that's him. He always played it cool, but I got the impression that he was actually very hotheaded under all the acting. He was condescending, and I always imagined him thinking of himself as the REAL hero, the one that would save the world because of what he knew about games.

"Now for Mr. Itsuki. News of your deeds has echoed throughout the land. You truly did an amazing job in such trying times. Your reward is 3,800 pieces of silver."

Itsuki sighed but seemed to consider the compensation just. Even still, I saw him cast a jealous glance in Motoyasu's direction.

His real name was Itsuki Kawasumi, and he was a year older than Ren, so 17 years old. He gave off an impression of softness and delicacy. And yet, there was an emptiness and vanity about him. He carried the Legendary Bow.

We hadn't spoken much, so I still didn't know very much about him. But he had the same sort of knowledge about the world that Ren and Motoyasu had, and I knew that he came from yet another Japan.

He looked like the youngest among us heroes. But in reality, Ren was the youngest.

Even still, what was this request that the king mentioned to Ren? It was the first I've heard of it.

"As for the Shield, we hope he will make more of an effort from now on."

He didn't even use my name! Who's this "Shield"?

I was so irritated I felt like I might snap. After the crap he pulled yesterday?

I reached out for my bag of money, but the attendant pulled it away before I could grab it.

"As a fee for the removal of the slavery curse placed on Raphtalia, your support funds will be revoked!"

The bastard!

"Um . . . My liege . . ."

Raphtalia raised her hand.

"What is it, demi-human?"

"What was this request you mentioned?"

So Raphtalia was trying to figure it out too. She ignored that our money was being taken away and approached it from another angle.

"The problems that plague our great nation are being dealt with, on my request, by the heroes."

"Why hasn't this same request been made of Mr. Naofumi? This is the first I've heard of this."

"Ha! What could the Shield hope to accomplish?"

Damn! I really hated this guy.

Everyone in the audience chamber started snickering.

Oh man . . . I couldn't stand it. I was about to explode.

" . . . "

I thought I was having a hard time, but I could actually hear how hard Raphtalia was balling her hands into fists.

I looked over, and she was nearly shaking with rage.

Okay, I think we can hold it in for now.

"Well, it's true that he didn't really help much."

"You're right. I didn't see him during the battle. I wonder what he was doing."

"If a hero won't throw himself into battle, I'm not sure what he's good for."

The remaining three heroes all added their ironic comments.

Now I was getting really annoyed. I had to say something.

"Sure, leaving all the villagers to die while you rush off to fight the boss—that's really saving the day, isn't it? Heroes?"

Right, they had ignored the groups of villagers that were in trouble and ran straight for a single enemy on the battlefield. Someone had to save the people, and that job fell to me.

"Ha! That's what the knights are for! Isn't it?"

"Yeah, the problem is that the knights are idiots! If I'd left them to the knights, how many people do you think would have died? You wouldn't even know because you were only looking at the boss!"

Motoyasu, Ren, and Itsuki all turned to look at the captain of the knights. The captain slowly nodded in irritation before speaking.

"But . . . If the Heroes aren't doing all they can to suppress the wave at its source, the destruction will only grow! Stop your foolish boasting!"

Ha! I couldn't believe my ears.

All he did was arrogantly lounge around the castle . . . And besides, was everyone forgetting that I was one of the heroes? Or what was this? Were they saying I wasn't the Shield Hero at all?

"All right, all right. Well, the rest of us are pretty busy, so we'll just be getting on our way now."

Getting in a fight now wouldn't do me any good. The best thing I could do was just leave quietly.

"Wait now, Shield."

"Huh? What is it now? Unlike some haughty king on his throne, I actually have things to do."

"You are even worse than I could have expected. Leave me! And do not ever show your face here again."

What the?! This Trash would go to any length to piss me off!

"Excellent news, don't you think? Mr. Naofumi?"

Raphtalia was grinning from ear to ear.

"What?"

"Now we don't have to waste our time in this place anymore. Instead of spending our time on trifles, now we can dedicate ourselves to something of worth."

"Y . . . Yeah."

I was starting to feel like I could really depend on her.

She took my hand in hers and squeezed it. She must have been angry too. It felt like we had so much anger between us, anger we couldn't handle on our own. But together . . .

"Wait just a moment."

Itsuki threw his hand in the air and spoke to Trash.

"What is it, Bow Hero?"

What was he up to? Not like I could expect him to say anything that made any sense at all.

"About the duel last night. Mr. Naofumi was treated unfairly, as someone intervened from behind. What are you planning to do about that? That's basically what I wanted to ask."

For a split second, the room went silent.

"I'm not sure what you mean."

"Well, the duel was originally over Ms. Raphtalia's freedom. Despite the clear evidence that the duel was not fair, Ms. Raphtalia's slavery curse was still removed. Now this was supposed to be payment for losing the duel, correct? And yet, you have also revoked Mr. Naofumi's payment under the pretext of payment for the curse removal. I'm asking if you think that is a just arrangement."

What's this now? Itsuki's eyes were sharp, and he was speaking out, strongly, against the king?

"He's right. I was watching from up above, and according

to the rules, if it was a fair match, Naofumi should have won."

"I didn't lose!"

Motoyasu shouted, but Ren and Itsuki were not listening to his protest. Their eyes were cold.

"Depending on your answer, we might need to reconsider whether Naofumi is even guilty of the crimes he's been accused of."

"I . . . Well . . ."

Trash sat there, his eyes moving over the crowd, dumbfounded.

"Oh, it wasn't like that at all! Mr. Itsuki, Mr. Ren! You've got it all wrong!"

Bitch was all decked out in fine clothes and a thick smear of makeup. She pushed her way through the crowd.

That's right! It was all her, the woman that framed me and dragged my name through the mud: it was the Bitch!

Myne Suphia. Apparently her real name was Malty, but who cares about her stupid name?

Like her personality, her hair was dark red, and she had an obnoxious, scheming air about her. Even still, I had to admit that she was pretty.

When we'd first set out adventuring, nobody volunteered to go with me but her. But she ended up stealing all of the money I'd been provided before framing me for a crime, ruining my reputation, and running to Motoyasu's side. She was pure evil.

So I'd made up my mind to call her Bitch from that point on.

And would you believe it? Bitch just happens to be the princess too.

The book I was reading back in my own world, *The Records of the Four Holy Weapons*, also spoke of a bitchy princess. I was pretty sure that it had been talking about her.

"The duel was supposed to be one-on-one, and yet the Shield Hero hid monsters under his cape to use against his opponent. This is a clear violation of the rules, and therefore my father, the king, has made a wise ruling."

Give me a break. How could he expect me to fight when I wasn't even capable of attacking?! They must have known that when they challenged me to a duel.

"I understand how you feel, and yet . . ."

"You just can't agree?"

Itsuki and Ren looked disappointed.

Bitch was obviously trying to think of another way out of it. Her brain only worked when she was plotting against someone else.

"Ms. Myne. Even if what you say is true, your own actions also constitute a violation of the rules."

"Sure, he hasn't been working as hard as the rest of us, but from what I could tell the guild hasn't given him any work either. Doesn't he need at least a little support, just to survive?

Besides, he really did protect the villagers during the wave when the knights didn't do anything."

Bitch's face twisted up. I could tell she was annoyed.

What could she do? Sure, she could use her authority as the princess, but she knew she couldn't get away with obviously manipulating the heroes.

The burden of proof should be on her. This was different from the time they framed me. There hadn't been any witnesses back then.

"Very well then. We will provide him with a small amount of funds. Take them and be gone."

Trash gave his pompous order from on high, and an attendant tossed a bag of money in my direction.

"Very well then, my liege. We will take our leave. Thank you for your judicious consideration."

Raphtalia sounded cheerful, and she led me out of the castle.

"Running off with his tail between his legs."

As if Motoyasu had any room to talk. Ren and Itsuki stood by in silence.

Who knew? Just acknowledging our mutual hatred made life so much easier.

Besides, it was starting to seem like Ren and Itsuki were harboring their own doubts about Motoyasu. Even still, they weren't going to do anything about it. They wouldn't sacrifice their own position, now would they? Nah . . . They'd have to stay on my blacklist for now.

"All right then, let's head back to the slave trader's tent and have him reapply the slave curse."

"What?"

Raphtalia said this to me immediately after exiting the castle gates.

"If we don't, I don't think you'll ever be able to really believe me, from the bottom of your heart."

"I don't . . . C'mon, you don't need to be a slave anymore."

"I think I do."

"What?"

"Mr. Naofumi, you've lost the ability to believe in anyone who is not your slave. Don't you lie to me about it either."

Had I done a bad job raising her?

She was right that I couldn't believe in anyone who wasn't a slave, but still, I think I could believe in her, even if she wasn't a slave.

If Raphtalia had only been thinking of herself, then she would have run to Motoyasu after the duel. That would have been best for her.

She knew that everyone in the kingdom hated me, and that no one trusted me. And yet she still chose to team up with me. That said something.

"Hey, Raphtalia . . ."

"What is it?"

"You really don't need to get the curse."

"But I want it."

What was wrong with this girl?

"I want proof that you believe in me."

When she said that, I instantly thought that I wanted to protect her.

Emotion welled up in my chest. I think it was love, but there was something else there too.

She certainly looked like a full-grown woman, but she'd been a child only a week or two prior. Apparently demi-humans matured by level as opposed to age.

She had lost her parents in a wave of destruction only recently. Maybe the emotion I was feeling wasn't romantic love—no, I think it was more like the love of a parent. I must have felt that way because I'd seen her grow up before my own eyes. Yes, that had to be it.

That must be what it feels like to be a parent. That would be my role. I had to watch over her.

"C'mon, let's go."

If she was that insistent on it, then I wasn't going to be able to stop her. She could do whatever she wanted.

We decided to pay a visit to that tent, the one that was selling slaves.

Chapter One: Egg Machine

"Well, well, if it isn't the hero! What can I do for you to-day?"

We entered the tent, and the courteous slave trader was right there to meet us.

"Whoa . . ."

He looked Raphtalia over carefully and grunted in surprise.

"She's certainly changed. Who thought she was such a diamond in the rough?"

He looked over at me and sighed.

He was the slave trader that had met me at my darkest hour. Just as I had all my possessions stolen and reputation ruined, just when I realized I had to level up without any means of attack, he showed up and asked if I might be interested in a slave.

He was an older man, plump, and decked out in a suit with coattails. He looked untrustworthy, to say the least.

But he took a liking to me for some reason and said he would do what he could to help. He was the man who sold me Raphtalia.

"What?"

"I thought she was more like us. I hadn't realized she had so much potential."

What the hell was that supposed to mean? I almost blew up at him but managed to control myself.

I didn't want to ruin our relationship. Who knew when I might need his services in the future? I'd say something along those lines.

"Whether they live or die, the proper way to use a slave is the way that raises the quality of the product."

I responded in a threatening tone.

"I guess all the slaves you know of are disposable?"

"N . . . Naofumi?"

She was looking at me, worried that I wasn't showing proper respect to authority.

I was aware of it myself, that I was a little out of control. But I was feeling better than I had the last time I met him.

"Heh, heh, heh . . . I suppose so. You've got me trembling."

I couldn't tell if he liked my answer or not, but he was smiling.

"Now then, as for the appraisal. She certainly has become a beauty, but if she's not a virgin, then I would say . . . 20 pieces of gold?"

"Why are you assuming he's here to sell me?! And besides, I AM a virgin!"

He jumped back at the force of her exclamation.

"Now we're talking! How does 30 pieces of gold sound? Naturally, I'll have to confirm your virginity."

"Mr. Naofumi!"

I could get 30 pieces of gold for Raphtalia?

"Mr. Naofumi! Please say something!"

If I had 30 pieces of gold, I could easily buy that level 75 Wolf Man!

I was thinking it over when Raphtalia shot me a terrified look before grabbing onto my shoulders.

"Mr. Naofumi, if you don't stop playing around, I'll get angry!"

"What is it? Why are you so upset?"

"This guy is sizing me up, and you aren't saying anything about it."

"We have to look nonchalant or we'll lose face."

That's all I could think of to get her off of my back. If I didn't hide my thoughts better, Raphtalia would figure out what I was thinking. And besides, it's not like I would sell off the only person that believed in me.

And yet . . .

"Thirty pieces of gold . . .?"

I caught myself muttering, and Raphtalia gripped my shoulders even harder.

"Ouch! Ouch!"

It looked like Raphtalia's attack power was now stronger than my own defense.

That was good. I could depend on that in battle.

"You want me to just run away? Right now?"

"I'm just kidding. I was just surprised that you are worth that much."

"But . . . But Mr. Naofumi . . ."

She relaxed her grip and looked embarrassed.

"Anyway, Slave Trader, I've already decided not to sell her. Who would sell off their own daughter?"

"Daughter?"

"Don't worry about it."

"Huh . . .?"

Even if I behaved like her father, she really only had two actual parents. If I just started behaving like her father, she was sure to hate it.

"Well, that is too bad. Too bad indeed . . . Now then, what can I do for you?"

"Haven't you heard all the commotion at the castle?"

He smiled at the question.

"I've heard of it. The slave curse has been lifted, yes?"

"If you already know, then that makes things easier. And if you already know, then don't waste our time appraising her worth."

I'd been on the verge of losing my good graces with her.

"That king's rash remarks are not going to get rid of slavery in this kingdom. No sir."

The previous night, the king was so upset that I was

keeping Raphtalia as a slave that he was going to bend the laws to confiscate her. Apparently the only justification was that Motoyasu didn't like the idea of it.

"Huh? But the royal family doesn't keep slaves, do they?"

"Ha! The royals buy more slaves than anyone. They find all sorts of ways to put them to use. Yes sir."

"That idiot Motoyasu! The stupid Spear Hero, did he think that he could say all those things and not end up a hypocrite against the Crown?"

Come to think of it, that really would be hilarious, and it would probably be better for the country in the end.

"Yes, the country is not monolithic. There are many different voices to be heard. If the Crown were to speak out against it, they would be the first ones to suffer from the proclamation. Yes sir."

"Does the fool really have that much power?"

Yes, the monarchy exercised absolute authority—but that doesn't mean it can do whatever it wants. If the Crown acts against the wishes of the people, there will be riots. Under such circumstances, the royal family may not be able to hold on to power for very long. His little princess wouldn't be too happy about losing her shot at the throne.

"Yes, well, there are people with more power than the king . . ."

"Um . . . What about the slave curse? Did we forget about that?"

"Oh, yes, right away."

The conversation got derailed a little. And besides, if we weren't going to see Trash anymore, who cared?

"Yes, so you've come to have the curse reapplied, correct?"

"Yeah, can you do it?"

"Naturally."

He snapped his fingers, and a servant appeared with the same jar that we had used for the ceremony the last time.

Raphtalia looked ashamed as she removed her breastplate and exposed her chest.

"H . . . How is it?"

"What?"

Raphtalia sighed.

Huh? Why did she look so upset?

And why was she sighing? Did I do something wrong?

Just like the last time, they mixed my blood with some ink and painted the curse seal onto Raphtalia's chest. The pattern began to shine and glow.

"Ugh . . ."

She grit her teeth in pain.

The slave icon reappeared in my field of vision. A window detailing the rules of use also appeared.

I suppose I didn't need to read it as thoroughly as I had the last time. Raphtalia had become a slave once again to earn my trust. I needed to believe in her too. Honestly, she really didn't need to bother with the whole ceremony. It was just a show.

"Now then."

I started mulling over the next steps to take when I noticed the pot of ink.

I reached out to touch it, and my shield began to react.

"Hey, can I buy some of this ink off of you?"

"Certainly."

I poured the remaining ink onto the shield.

The shield absorbed the ink.

Slave User Shield: conditions met
Slave User Shield II: conditions met

Slave User Shield: ability locked: equip bonus: slave maturation adjustment (small)
Slave User Shield II: ability locked: equip bonus: slave status adjustment (small)

A Slave User Shield? Hm . . . well, I guess it only made sense.

I looked at the tree, and it appeared on its own, branching out from the very first small shield. Because of that, it wasn't very strong. But its equip bonuses seemed promising.

Maturation adjustment . . .

And hey, I'd only dumped a little ink on it, but I still ended up with two new shields.

So all I needed to do was equip the shield for a while to unlock the ability, and then I'd be able to use those equip bonuses forever. It was a great system. The Legendary Shield allowed me to equip all these different shield types, learn their abilities, and then keep the abilities as I moved on through the levels. That was why us heroes could grow stronger than just normal people: our skill tree continued to grow.

I think I had a pretty good handle on the skills, abilities, status boosts, and equip bonuses that the shield had accrued so far. But there were still so many things I didn't understand, and I was beginning to feel that my mastery of the shield would decide whether or not I survived.

I quietly looked over at Raphtalia.

"What is it?"

That reminds me. I'd let the shield absorb some of her hair. At the time I'd seen something about a raccoon shield, but this must have completed another requirement. That must be what unlocked the Slave User Shield II. At least, that was my best guess.

Which would mean that . . .

"Raphtalia, can I use a little of your blood?"

"What is it?"

"I want to try something."

She tilted her head and looked confused but poked the end of her finger with a penknife anyway. She dripped the blood into the ink pot, mixed it, and poured a little onto my shield.

Slave User Shield III: conditions met

Slave User Shield III: ability locked: equip bonus: slave maturation adjustment (medium)

Nice! I was right!

"Mr. Naofumi? You look like you're having a lot of fun over there."

"Yeah, well, I just unlocked an interesting-looking shield."

"Excellent."

I changed my shield into the Slave User Shield and decided to wait for the ability to unlock.

"Now then . . . Hm?"

We were finished there, so I turned to leave when I noticed a large wooden crate in the corner of the tent. It was filled with eggs.

I'd never seen it before. What could it be?

"What is that?"

I asked the slave trader.

"Oh, that's a product for our cover business."

"And what IS your cover business?"

"We deal in monsters."

His eyes shined when he answered.

"Monsters? You mean there are monster trainers around here?"

"You are a very clever man. Have you heard of them?"

"I don't think I've ever met one, but . . ."

"Mr. Naofumi."

Raphtalia raised her hand.

"What is it?"

"Filolials are monsters raised by monster trainers."

I'd never even heard of a Filolial. I didn't know what she was talking about.

"What's that?"

"Those giant birds around town. The ones that pull carriages instead of horses."

"Oh, yeah. Okay."

I'd seen them in town. They were giant birds that were used like horses. I thought they were some kind of animal that existed in this world, but I guess they were technically monsters.

"There was a monster trainer in my village. He had a ranch where he raised different monsters for their meat."

"Really . . ."

I guess in this world, farmers and ranch herders, anyone that worked with creatures like that, were considered monster trainers. Maybe they just didn't have the idea of "animal" and everything that wasn't human was called a monster.

"So what are those eggs?"

"If the monsters aren't raised from the egg, they won't take to human masters well. That is why we sell them as eggs. Yes sir."

"Okay."

"Would you like to see the monster cages?"

He'd sell anything you wanted. This slave trader was quite the capitalist.

"Nah, I'm good for now. But hey, what is that sign that's leaning on the egg crate?"

I couldn't read what was written on it, but there was an arrow pointing to the box, and it appeared to be scrawled with numbers.

"It's a lottery! One try for 100 pieces of silver, and if you win, you get an egg!"

"That's one expensive ticket."

At the moment, we had 508 pieces of silver, which was quite a lot of money.

"Well, they are very valuable monsters."

"I'm just asking to get an idea, but what were they called? Filolials? How much do you normally sell one of those for?"

"For an adult? Typically around 200 pieces, but that can go up or down depending on the quality. Yes sir."

"If you charge 200 pieces for an adult, then I'm guessing a chick is cheaper? And the eggs must be even cheaper yet . . . Well, I suppose you have to account for the cost of raising the thing, but still. I'm wondering if it's a good deal."

"Well it's not like that, you see. The real egg is mixed in with other eggs."

"Oh yeah, you did call it a lottery."

So you could either hit or miss.

So if you pulled a loser, you would get nothing, and if you pulled a winner, you still ended up paying more than you would have in the first place.

"And I'm guessing there aren't actually any real eggs in there?"

"How dare you. Are you accusing me of unjust business practices? My dear hero . . ."

"Am I wrong?"

"I am very proud of my business. I might enjoy tricking a customer now and then, but I take no pleasure from misrepresenting my products."

"You like tricking people but not misrepresentation?"

I couldn't follow his logic. I gave up on that for the time being.

"And what do you get if you pull the winning egg?"

"I'll try to make it easy for you to understand, being a foreigner and all. Simply put: a Knight's Dragon."

Whoa, a Knight's Dragon? I wonder if that was a class of dragon that knights rode in battle.

"Is that a dragon that people ride like a horse?"

"Not just that. This one can fly. They are very popular, so the game has been a hit with the nobility."

"A flying dragon? It was like a dream!"

"Mr. Naofumi?"

"To buy one on the market, you'd need around 20 pieces of gold. They are one of the cheaper dragons. Yes sir."

"What's the probability? Just tell me the chances for the dragon egg."

"There are 250 eggs in the crate, and only one of them is a dragon egg."

So it was a 1/250 chance.

"I've compensated for differences in weight with a magical spell. You must agree to the possibility of drawing a losing egg before purchasing a ticket."

"You're quite the businessman."

"Yes, well. Whenever there is a winner, I learn their name, and they tend to spread the word around for me."

"Yeah, but those chances aren't so great . . ."

"Well, there is this box over here, and if you buy ten tickets, you are guaranteed to win at least once. Yes sir."

"Well, I assume there are no dragon eggs in that one?"

"Yes, that's true, but the prize is definitely worth at least 300 pieces of silver."

Hold on a second. Isn't this like some online slot machine? C'mon!

These games are set up to make profits for the businesses who make them. And he almost had me for a second there . . .

"Hmm . . ."

Thinking it over, I wondered how far I could progress with only Raphtalia in my party.

Would it be cheaper to buy another slave or to buy a monster to travel with us?

Maybe I should try out my new slave user shield. Raphtalia was already at a pretty high level, so the maturation adjustment probably wouldn't benefit her all that much.

But then again, I'd have to raise the monster. When I was traveling with Raphtalia, the major costs were updating her equipment. But there was a good chance that monsters could fight without having to use any equipment at all. I could use all the additional money we earned on Raphtalia.

"All right, I'll try it once."

"Thank you very much! As a show of good will, I'll excuse the cost of the slave curse ceremony."

"How generous of you. I like that kind of thing."

"Mr. Naofumi?!"

"What is it?"

"Are you buying a monster egg?"

"Yeah, I thought we could probably use another party member. I could get a slave, but they would end up costing more money for equipment. I figured that investing in a monster might be a good way to go."

"Yes, but monsters can be a real handful."

"I know that. But don't you kind of want a pet?"

"Are you sure that you aren't trying to get a dragon egg?"

"Even if we got an Usapil, I'd be fine with that."

I kind of liked little animals. MMORPGs often let you keep pets and use them in your party. At the very least, they could be relaxing to have around. And if I could give them orders, like a slave, then they could help out in battle.

We had a little extra money, and I could tell that it was loosening my purse strings. But still, it didn't seem like a poor investment to me. Besides, if there was a Slave Shield, there should be one for monsters too.

"And if we raise it up and then sell it, we won't feel as bad as if we'd done the same thing to a slave."

"Oh, okay, I think I understand now."

Sure, we might get attached, but we needed money—there was no escaping that.

I think selling off a slave is difficult because you know that they are a person. Just like Raphtalia had come back to me of her own free will, if the next slave did the same thing, I wasn't sure I'd even be able to sell another slave off at all. At least a monster wouldn't talk. So even if we did grow attached, I think I'd still be able to turn it over for a profit.

I could just pass it over and sort of pray that it ends up with a good master. Something like that anyway.

"I'm sure you'd assist me in that, wouldn't you?"

"The depth of your consideration never fails to impress, Hero. Yes sir!"

He was loving this conversation.

I looked over at all the eggs. He already said that there was a spell on them to make them indistinguishable, so I guess I should just choose one at random.

"I'll take that one."

I just followed my intuition and chose one from the right side of the line.

"Look at the symbol painted on the eggshell and copy it onto the dish before you."

I did as he said and painted the symbol onto the dish. When I did, the symbol glowed red, and a new icon appeared in my field of vision. It said monster training. Just like when the slave icon originally appeared, a window also showed up detailing various rules of usage that I could set for the monster.

I selected the option that it would have to obey my orders or face punishment. I decided to make the punishment more severe than what I had set for Raphtalia. That seemed the obvious choice—this was a monster after all. I wasn't sure if it understood language, so I would have to make sure to put a lot of emotion into my voice when I scolded it. The thing wasn't even hatched yet though.

The slave trader wrung his hands in delight and brought

over a machine that looked like some kind of incubator. I placed the egg inside.

"If it doesn't hatch, I'll be back for my money."

"I tip my hat to you, Hero! Determined to get his money's worth even if he pulled a losing egg."

The slave trader seemed to be in a very good mood. Was he some sort of closeted masochist? Not that I wanted to make fun of another guy, but . . . actually, come to think of it, I wouldn't mind seeing those other stupid heroes in a bit of pain.

"Even if it's just a verbal agreement, I really will be back. If you act like this conversation never happened, my unstable slave here might just cause a ruckus."

"Hey, what are you expecting me to do?"

"I'll be waiting for you. Yes sir!"

He was in a VERY good mood.

"Just when should I expect it to hatch?"

I passed him 100 pieces of silver as I asked.

"It's written on the incubator."

"Let's see here . . ."

I saw something that looked like numbers of some kind, but I couldn't read them.

"Raphtalia, can you read this?"

"Let's see. Just a little bit. It looks like the numbers will be gone sometime tomorrow."

"That's fast. Excellent."

I was getting excited. I couldn't wait to see what kind of monster hatched from the egg.

"I'm always glad when you pay me a visit. Yes sir."

I took the egg in my arms, and we turned, leaving the tent behind us.

Chapter Two: Gratitude for Life

So what was next?

I was wondering that very thing when I remembered the extra medicine I had left over from the wave of destruction. I'd made a whole bunch, just to be safe, but at this point it probably made more sense to sell off what I didn't need.

"Let's stop by the apothecary and then head to the weapon shop."

"Mr. Naofumi, take care that you don't get too careless with your money. If you keep doing things like you just did, you'll only make life harder on yourself."

"I know that."

"Our current equipment is just fine. Why bother thinking about it until you are sure that you need it?"

" . . ."

Well, I guess she had a point after all. But compared to the other heroes, we were using junk. I still thought that getting Raphtalia better equipment and then moving on to fight stronger monsters would be the best strategy . . .

"And besides, we just got new equipment a few days ago. Just imagine what the weapon shop owner would say."

"Yeah . . ."

She was right, the old guy had given us a lot of help. And he'd given us new equipment while including the trade-in value of our older stuff too. Whatever we got from him now probably wouldn't be substantially better than what we already had.

The weapon shop owner was the only person that had helped me out after those bastards framed me—I liked the guy. Everything we currently had equipped, Raphtalia's weapons and my own armor, we'd purchased from him.

So I wanted to keep patronizing him, and I wanted to pay him back for all he'd done.

"Fine. Let's save up for a while."

"Okay!"

Granted, it wasn't a BAD idea to buy new equipment after our wallets had gained a little weight.

"Okay, let's head to the apothecary."

I poked my head into the shop, and when the owner saw me, he let a smile play over his face.

"What? What is it?"

This guy normally looked pretty sullen, which I assumed was some kind of business strategy on his part. So what was he looking so happy for? It set my nerves on edge.

"Oh, not much. I've been waiting for you to stop by. Waiting for a chance to say thanks, you know?"

"For what?"

I looked to Raphtalia. Neither of us knew what he was talking about.

"I have some family in Riyute. They say that you saved them. They asked me to help you out if I ever ran into you."

"Hmm . . . You don't say."

The wave of destruction had occurred near a town called Riyute, where I'd based my operations for a time. In the midst of all the chaos, I'd dedicated my energies to the evacuation effort, and the town ended up fairing pretty well because of that. When the wave had passed, the Riyute villagers had all lined up and said thank you to me. Apparently this guy's relatives had been among them.

"So anyway, in thanks, I'd like to . . ."

The owner took a book off of the bookshelf behind him.

"What's that?"

"You sold me some lower-level potions earlier, which leads me to believe that those were the only recipes you knew. This book has better recipes, for mid-level potions. I think you are probably ready to take them on."

" . . . "

I hesitantly opened the book on the counter. It was pretty old, and the cover was well worn. Even still, I could only discern some of the characters written there.

But I couldn't read them.

"Th . . . Thank you. I'll do my best."

He'd gone out of his way to be nice to me, so I didn't want to let it go without at least saying thanks. The book probably contained recipes for medicines that would sell for a good price.

"I'm glad to hear you say that."

Ugh . . . I hated the pressure of having to respond to people's kindness. I'd given up on trying to read it since I didn't understand the language they used to write things around here. I suppose I should make a more sincere effort.

"The owner of the magic shop wanted you to stop by too."

"Magic shop?"

"Mr. Naofumi? It's a shop that sells books to teach magical spells."

"Oh, I see."

I'd seen the shop in town but had assumed it was a bookstore. Thinking back on it then, I remembered seeing a crystal ball in the back of the shop.

"Where's the shop?"

"Right on the main street. You can't miss it."

Yes, I remember seeing it. It was the biggest or second biggest bookstore in town—I mean magic shop.

"Excellent. So what can I do for you today?"

"I was hoping you would . . ."

He ended up buying the medicine off of me for a better price than I'd gotten yet.

I bought some new materials with the money and went looking for the magic shop.

"Oh! The Shield Hero! I have to thank you for saving my grandchild."

"Right . . ."

I didn't actually know who she was talking about, but it must have been one of the villagers in Riyute. The old lady who ran the shop had run to politely greet me at the door.

I call her an old lady, but she was a pudgy woman dressed like a witch.

"I heard you wanted to see me?"

I looked around the shop I'd previous misconstrued as a bookstore. The shelves were lined with old, dusty books, and there were a number of crystal balls lined up behind the counter. There were some staves and wands around—pretty much what you would expect for a magic shop.

Come to think of it though, I had no idea how you were supposed to learn magic.

"Before that, is this young lady your only traveling companion?"

"Huh? Oh . . . yeah."

I caught Raphtalia's gaze, and we both nodded.

"Then wait right there for a moment, please."

She went behind the counter, took a crystal ball off of the shelf, and began chanting a spell over it.

"Yes. Now then, Shield Hero, please look deep into the ball."

"Um . . . Okay."

I had no idea what to expect, but I looked deep into the ball.

Something was shining, but I couldn't really see anything in particular.

"Yes, yes, it seems that you, Shield Hero, are suited to learning recovery and support magic."

"Huh?"

Was she looking to see what kind of magic I was best suited to?

If only she'd told me earlier, I would have had some idea of what was going on . . . Oh well, it wasn't like I had any room to complain, but she could have explained herself a little better.

"Next I'll take a look at the nice young lady behind you."

"Yes, ma'am."

Raphtalia stepped forward and looked deep into the crystal ball.

"Yes, yes, that only makes sense. The young raccoon girl seems best suited for light and shadow magic."

"Why do you say that it only makes sense? Is that common knowledge?"

"Yes, the raccoon people are said to control phantoms that contain both the refractive properties of light and the indefinite properties of shadow."

I was starting to understand. They were like the raccoons

or *tanuki* of my own world. In my own Japan, people often said that *tanuki* were shapeshifting creatures that could take on human form. Apparently that way of thinking was something our universes had in common.

"Okay, so what is all this about?"

"Yes, well, this is what I was hoping to give you," the old lady said and handed us three books.

More books! I couldn't read them at all, not a single word, but everyone was showering me in books that day.

"I'd really like to give you a crystal ball, but if I did, I would put myself out of business . . ."

"Why's that?"

"Don't you know, Shield Hero? If you can free the magic that is sealed in a crystal ball, you'll learn it instantly."

What?! So I could learn to use magic even if I wasn't able to read the books?

"Quite a while ago, the country went ahead and ordered a large number of crystal balls for the four heroes. Haven't you heard anything about this?"

"Not a word."

Thanks to that Trash, no doubt. He must have given the crystal balls to the other heroes after I'd left.

He went out of his way to intentionally exclude me from everything . . . Ugh . . . Just thinking about it made me want to murder the man.

"The magic books are not an easy read—that's for sure. But if you apply yourself, you'll eventually be able to learn a good number of spells from those."

That was probably why there was only one crystal ball but a wide variety of magic books. Of course, they were only worth something if you were capable of reading them.

"I'm sorry . . ."

"Oh, don't be! Just getting these books will be a huge help!" Raphtalia smiled and answered. I nodded along.

"How much magic do you think we can learn from these?"

"Well, those are all books for beginners. For anything more advanced . . . Think I could ask you to purchase anything additional?"

"Oh, sure."

"I could probably teach you the spells myself, but the Shield Hero is very busy, is he not? I suppose you can't just hang around the castle town?"

"That's true."

She did have a business to run, after all. She was cutting into her own profits to give us these books, so it didn't seem right to complain about it.

"Thank you."

I said it in a rather difficult way, but we received the books she offered and left the magic shop.

"Geez . . ."

I sighed without thinking. I had never really liked studying, so what was I supposed to do now?

Anyone with half a brain knew that the best course of action would be to buckle down, learn to read, and then study the books to learn new recipes and magic.

Of course that's what they would say.

I found myself wondering if there was some skill I could equip to make it easier, something like "other world language translation." There might have been medicinal recipes stored in the shield somehow. If I looked for them, I might even find them. But what would end up taking more time? Learning to read or finding the shield that would give me the recipes directly?

The reading might be cheaper, but if you considered the time investment, it wouldn't be. And it would entail getting new materials to experiment with also.

I still kept coming back to the idea of the translation skill, and every time I thought of it, my desire to learn to read just shrunk even more.

"Let's study up on that magic!" Raphtalia said to me.

"But I don't know how to read the writing here . . ."

"I know. That's why we should do it together."

"Yeah . . . I suppose that only makes sense."

It did seem like a good idea to get some new recipes under my belt.

"That reminds me—how much time do we have until the next wave comes?"

"Huh? Oh, wait a second."

I referenced the icon in the corner of my field of vision.

Apparently this whole system was called "status magic" and everyone in this world could use it.

As for me, my attack rating was as low as possible, but my defense rating was through the roof.

Among the other icons there, there was another one that only the heroes could see. I focused my energies on it, and a clock appeared that indicated the amount of time remaining until the next wave was to arrive.

It looked like forty-five days and fourteen hours.

"Looks like we have forty-five whole days!"

So they didn't come every month?!

Well, it's not like we had two months or anything, but that reminds me of something: we hadn't been summoned here until after the first wave had already come. That meant that the frequency could be different than we had previously thought. If I thought about all the time I'd spent on my own before I teamed up with Raphtalia, it seemed to add up.

Over one month left some room for interpretation.

"Well, having extra time is a good thing."

And if I thought about all the preparations we really should be making, it wasn't exactly like we had time to spare.

"Anyway, are we done here, for now?"

"I think so. Let's see. We reapplied the slave curse, sold our extra medicines, and got those books from the magic shop. That should be it."

I went over it all with Raphtalia. If we forgot something and had to come back, we'd just lose that much time.

"Then let's get some breakfast and go level up."

"Okay."

I was surprised with the meal. My sense of taste had finally returned.

I'd nearly forgotten how delicious food could be. It was invigorating.

Mortar Shield: conditions met
Beaker Shield: conditions met
Druggist's Mortar Shield: conditions met

Mortar Shield: ability locked: equip bonus: new compounding

Beaker Shield: ability locked: equip bonus: liquid compounding bonus
Druggist's Mortar shield: ability locked: equip bonus: collection skill 2

We finished our meals and decided to leave the castle town and make our way to Riyute. There should be some monsters along the way that were perfect for leveling up at our current levels. Unlike the other heroes, I didn't already know where the best leveling-up and hunting spots were. So I either needed to find them myself or ask around and see what I could get other people to tell me.

I opened the map and gave it a quick look-over. There didn't seem to be anywhere that was very convenient, but it seemed like there were a few spots that would work well enough for our purposes. Granted, it wasn't a race—but even still, the idea of falling behind the other heroes grated on my nerves. And besides, fighting an unknown monster, and winning, would get me new skills and shields to work with. It didn't seem like a bad idea.

I've neglected to explain myself fully. There are a bunch of different forms my shield can take, and they all have different abilities. Unfortunately, most of them were just status and ability boosts, so they weren't a ton of help at the moment.

They were mostly defense boosts because I was working with a shield . . . at least that was my theory. Even still, aside from defense boosts, my agility, stamina, magic, and SP ratings, everything except for attack, were rising as well. That was how I was able to make it through the last wave unscathed.

We were walking down the road.

"You know, I wonder if I could absorb the enemies from the wave into my shield."

We'd left in a big hurry, so I hadn't even thought to try it. But I definitely wanted to try it now, as I needed to do whatever I could to make my shield stronger.

We were approaching the fields around Riyute, and there were dead enemies from the wave lying around here and there.

Inter-Dimensional Locust Shield: conditions met
Inter-Dimensional Lower Bee Shield: conditions met
Inter-Dimensional Zombie Shield: conditions met

Inter-Dimensional Locust Shield: ability locked: equip bonus: defense 6
Inter-Dimensional Lower Bee Shield: ability locked: equip bonus: agility 6
Inter-Dimensional Zombie Shield: ability locked: equip bonus: inventory rot resistance (small)

I butchered the enemies further to see if any of their parts would result in additional shields.

But apparently there wasn't enough of the materials remaining for most of them, and I was only able to unlock one more.

Bee Needle Shield: conditions met

Bee Needle Shield: ability locked: equip bonus: attack 1

Special Effect: Needle Shield (small), Bee Poison (paralysis)

I figured that was pretty much what I'd expected, and we continued on to the village. On the way, we came across a group of villagers removing a chimera's corpse.

"Hey."

"Oh! The Shield Hero."

No doubt thanks to what we'd been through during the wave, the villagers greeted me warmly.

"Was this guy the boss from the wave?"

I looked at the size of the body and felt sweat drip down my forehead.

I don't know how to describe it. It was a chimera, but there was something about it that made it look different than the other monsters I'd encountered in this world. I don't know if it was the coloring or some other more biological characteristic. It was hard to describe in concrete terms.

"It's a terrible thing."

"It sure is."

I agreed with what they were saying. It looked like the other heroes and knights had torn the thing apart for materials. The basic shape was still intact, but the skin and flesh were torn to shreds in places.

"Can I have a little of it?"

"Of course. We were just wondering what we should do with it. We were going to bring it back to the village and process it into equipment. Sound good?"

"Not a bad idea, but it doesn't look like there is anything of use left."

The skin was all ripped up, so they couldn't make any good armor from it. Still, they might be able to find a use for the flesh and bones and maybe the snake tail.

The head hadn't been cut off. It looked like there were three heads, and yet . . .

Raphtalia and I set to work butchering the remains and letting the shield absorb whatever it could.

Chimera Meat Shield: conditions met
Chimera Bone Shield: conditions met
Chimera Leather Shield: conditions met
Chimera Viper Shield: conditions met

Chimera Meat Shield: ability locked: equip bonus: cooking quality improvement
Chimera Bone Shield: ability locked: equip bonus: shadow resistance (medium)

Chimera Leather Shield: ability locked: equip bonus: defense 10

Chimera Viper Shield: ability locked: equip bonus: skill: Change Shield, Antidote Compounding Up, Poison Resistance (medium)

Special Effect: Snake Venom Fang (medium), Hook

The last one seemed to have a lot of good bonuses, and the defense rating was pretty high.

But to equip it, it looked like you needed to be at a pretty high level, and on top of that, you needed to have a lot of other chimera shields unlocked. I wouldn't be able to use it for a little while, but I got the feeling that it would be my main shield by the time the next wave arrived.

"What are you doing with the rest?"

"We were just going to bury it, so take whatever you like."

"Hm . . ."

It felt like it was going to waste somehow, but still . . . it looked like there was only flesh and bones left. The bones should keep just fine, but the meat? I couldn't think of anything to do with it but dry it out and make jerky. Not that it looked like it would taste good.

But hey, I bet they could be materials for some kind of magical potion, but even if they could be, who would buy them from me? I had no idea. They'd give me trouble if they started rotting, and what if I stored them improperly and it came back to life or something?

Sure, the same could be said about the bones, but I still felt better about them than I did about the meat. At the same time, what was I so worried about?

"All right, we'll take what we can carry."

"There's quite a lot though, Hero."

"You'll let me store it in the village, won't you?"

"Well, if that is your request, Hero . . ."

"You can hang up the meat to dry. If someone who wants it stops by, go ahead and sell it. But set aside a little for me. It might make you enough money to rebuild. If the meat and bones came from the wave of destruction, there must be some people who will want to study it. You could make some money that way."

"I suppose you are right, Hero."

The villagers wanted money to rebuild, so they followed my instructions.

I let the shield absorb the guts and anything that looked like it would rot quickly. Then we set off for the village. When we arrived, dusk was already on us.

The village was half-destroyed, and the remaining villagers were all living in the relatively unaffected buildings. The village chief prepared a room for us in the inn, which seemed to be in relatively good shape, and so we were able to get a good rest that night.

"I'd like to stick around and help them rebuild, but I don't think we have the time to spend worrying about all this."

The villagers were doing all they could to take care of us. I could understand being grateful for my help in disposing of the chimera corpse, but I didn't know how to feel about the free room and board.

"I know how you feel. I sure wish we could do something to help them all."

Some of the literate villagers drafted me a table of characters so that I might learn how to read their language.

It was something like the AIUEO tables in Japanese or the alphabet in English.

Later that night, I got Raphtalia's help, as she could read a little. I had her pronounce each character so that I could compare it to my own language. Then I drafted the answers, in my own language, onto the chart.

I imagined that they combined characters to make words, so any translation work would be hard-going, even though it wouldn't be impossible.

I sat down to work on some medicines, and while I was working, I struggled to memorize all their strange symbols.

Chapter Three: Filo

We slept in the next day since Raphtalia had stayed up pretty late the night before. She'd held the magic book in one hand and muttered to herself until the wee hours of the night. Me? I spent the night roasting herbs to make medicines.

I wanted to make up for lost time, so I was hurrying through my morning preparations. I wanted to get out on the road.

"Oh! It looks like it's going to hatch!"

I'd set the egg we'd bought by the window for the night, and Raphtalia had noticed a fine crack down the side.

You could just see something through the crack, something soft, like feathers or fur.

"Is it . . .?"

I was interested to see what hatched so I went over to have a look.

The cracks spread and opened with an audible crackle, and a baby monster's face popped through the hole.

"Cheep!"

It was like a small pink chick. It was covered in soft feathers, and there was a piece of eggshell still sitting on its head like a hat. It looked at me.

"Cheep!"

It chirped and suddenly flew up at me, bouncing into my face. It didn't hurt at all, but I was surprised the thing was so energetic, having just been born and all.

"What is this monster called? It looks like a bird. Is it a PikyuPikyu?"

PikyuPikyu were liked deformed little condors that couldn't fly very well. The monster looked like it could have been a baby PikyuPikyu. It did have a sharp beak though, so I could expect better attacks from it than I could have from a balloon or something.

"Oh . . . you know, I don't really know all that much about monsters . . ."

Raphtalia looked just as confused as I did.

"Fine then. Let's go ask the villagers if they know what it is."

If it was a monster that was approved for sale at a shop, it couldn't have been very dangerous. If I asked, I could probably get an answer out of someone. I reached out my hand for the little bird, and it hopped onto my palm, then flew to my shoulder and finally jumped up on my head.

"Cheeeeeeep!"

It kept cheeping and rubbing its face against mine. It was kind of cute.

"Oh, look! It thinks you are its parent, Mr. Naofumi."

"Must be some kind of imprinting."

I'd already registered it on my status screen, and I was the first thing it saw after it was born. I suppose it was only natural that it thought I was its father.

I decided to clean up the shards of eggshell, and when I did my shield began to react to them. Come to think of it, if I let the shield absorb them, it might tell me what kind of monster I was dealing with. So I held up a piece of eggshell and let the shield absorb it.

Monster User Shield: conditions met
Monster Egg Shield: conditions met

Monster User Shield: ability locked: equip bonus: monster maturation adjustment (small)
Monster Egg Shield: ability locked: equip bonus: cooking skill 2

It wasn't exactly what I had been expecting. But it still looked like it would be useful, so I switched my shield from Slave User Shield II (which I'd been using to unlock its ability) to the Monster User Shield.

"Did you figure it out?"

"No, it unlocked something else."

I still didn't know what kind of monster this chick was. I sure hoped the villagers could tell me something about it.

We set out walking around the half-ruined village, and I started thinking about where a good place to level up might be.

The most efficient place, considering our levels, was probably the swamp area to the west of the village. The last time we had been in the area we went to the mountains in the north, so I was hoping to find another place to go. I spotted some passing villagers, and they called out to me.

"Hello there, Shield Hero."

"Morning."

"Good morning!"

All in all, I'd spent about a week there, and after I protected them all during the wave, I guess most of them had come to recognize me.

One of them bowed very deeply to me, which I found awkward.

"Cheep!"

The little chick on my head chirped out a greeting of its own.

"What's that?"

The villagers all looked at the bird on my head.

"What happened?"

They pointed their fingers at the bird and asked in unison.

"I bought an egg from a monster trainer."

"Ah, gotcha."

"Do you know what kind of monster this is?"

They leaned in to get a better look.

"Hmm . . . Yes . . . I think it looks like a Filolial. Don't you think so?"

"The big birds that pull the carriages?"

If they were right, that meant that I had still made a little return on my investment—considering how much it would cost to buy a Filolial. If they were right . . .

"Well I'm not completely sure, but there is a small ranch at the edge of town. You might want to stop by and ask over there."

"Good idea. Let's go."

Raphtalia and I found out where the manager of the ranch lived and decided to stop by his house.

Apparently the ranch had been hit pretty hard during the wave, and he had lost more than half of the monsters he had been raising.

"Okay, but is this little thing actually a Filolial?" I asked the man there, and he nodded.

"Yes, it certainly does look like a baby Filolial."

He held the chick in his hand and only answered after he carefully looked it over.

"Yes, it is a very common variety of Filolial, but they have trouble staying calm without a cart to pull."

"What kind of a way to raise a monster is that?"

"Why, does it sound strange?"

Hmmm . . . I guess if you had been born and raised here, you wouldn't find things like this mysterious.

Come to think of it, it might have been that the monster had a natural desire to protect its nest or its eggs and that the monster trainers had just taught the monsters to fix their protective desire on carts instead.

"Well I guess it's not a loss then. Kind of a win, really."

If adults sold for 200 pieces of silver, and I was able to buy a baby for 100 pieces of silver, then it wasn't really a bad deal at all.

"Cheep!"

The baby Filolial was chirping from its perch on my head.

"What does this thing eat?"

"You should start her on cooked beans mushed into a puree. Something soft. Once she grows up, they aren't picky. They'll pretty much eat anything once they are adults."

"Gotcha. Thanks."

I even surprised myself at how quick and sincere my thanks were, because honestly, up until now I'd sort of considered everyone in this world to be my enemy. I was feeling better these days though. I wonder if it was because of what Raphtalia did for me back at the castle.

Anyway, they were selling boiled beans back at the village, so I might as well pick some up.

"What should we name it?"

Raphtalia was petting the little chick when she asked.

"Why do we have to give it a name? We might end up selling it, you know?"

If we went around naming things, we might get attached. That would only make it harder to sell the thing if that was what we decided to do in the future.

"Are you just going to call it 'chick' and 'Filolial'?"

"Hm . . ."

She was right. That would make things harder than they needed to be.

"You're right. Why don't we call it Filo?"

"Very creative."

"Oh, give me a break."

"Cheep!"

The little bird let out a loud and satisfied chirp, as if it understood that we had given it a name.

We thanked the rancher and left. Then we bought some boiled beans, had lunch for ourselves, and set out on the road.

"Where are we off to today?"

"Cheep?"

"Right, well, I don't really know anywhere around here that is good for leveling up, so I guess we will just have to search for ourselves. Let's just do what we've done the whole time."

"Okay."

Now that I knew I could depend on Raphtalia, I felt like the battles would be easier than they had been.

Filo was chirping from where it sat on my head. It was loud, but I kind of liked it.

"It's huge! That frog is huge!"

We'd gone to the swamplands to the west of Riyute to hunt monsters, but I wasn't able to hide my surprise at the first one I saw.

But let's be fair here. You might run into giant toads or something when you play an RPG, but if you saw one in real life, you'd be pretty surprised too.

So when this giant frog, "Big Frog" they're called, hopped over to me and I saw that it was as tall as my waist, I screamed.

"I'm going!"

"Wait! Raphtalia!"

Before I could restrain the Big Frog, Raphtalia jumped ahead of me.

When it came time to battle, we had agreed that I was to take the lead. If this was an MMORPG, it only made sense to do so because it was dangerous to approach a new monster when you didn't know its stats. What if the thing was stronger than we were?

If it was, we might not get out with just scrapes and bruises. It might be a mistake we'd have to pay for with our lives.

"Hiya!"

Raphtalia ignored my cry and dashed at the Big Frog with her sword.

The Big Frog let out a deafening screech, as if her attack had surprised it.

Dammit! What was she thinking? What happened to our plan? I was supposed to go in first and hold the monster down for her!

The Big Frog puffed up its cheeks and then sent its razor-sharp tongue flying at Raphtalia.

"Watch out!"

I ran forward and caught the brunt of the attack with my shield.

I couldn't allow Raphtalia to be injured.

"Cheep!"

Filo was excited on my head. It felt like the thing was running in circles, shadow boxing.

"I'll hold it down, so you just calm down!"

"But I . . ."

"Quiet!"

What was going on? It was like Raphtalia and I were not on the same page. I'd never felt that way prior to the wave. What could it mean?

If Raphtalia were to end up hurt, I'd feel terrible. I'd feel like we weren't honoring the memory of her parents. I'd made up my mind to protect her, to serve as her new father.

The Big Frog turned to me and sent its razor-sharp tongue flying in my direction.

Yes! I reached out and grabbed the tongue from the air. It made a sound like metal clanging against my fist.

"Go!"

"Okay!"

Raphtalia lunged at the frog with her sword drawn, her eyes flashing, like she'd just been waiting for my signal.

The Big Frog fell quickly and easily, and we both received experience points.

Nice. It was worth more than the porcupines had been.

"Huff."

Raphtalia was looking me over, and she seemed disappointed. Her tenacity was starting to get the better of her, and I'd have to say something about it. If she didn't learn to hold herself back a little, then we might both end up dead.

"Raphtalia, let's be a little more cautious . . . okay?"

"But we don't have much time until the next wave comes. Shouldn't we defeat as many enemies as we can? Shouldn't we level up as much as we possibly can?"

"We have a month and a half. That's plenty of time. Let's take it slow. You don't want to overdo it and end up bedridden, do you?"

"You're right. But I . . . I want to be stronger!"

At least she agreed with me . . . Wait. Did she?

I didn't know where all the good monsters were, like the other heroes did. So we didn't have any other options for efficient leveling up.

"Gugeeeeeeh!"

What the . . .? I turned at the sudden sound and saw something twice the size of the Big Frog. It was a purple Big Frog, and there was a Gray Salamander with it—and they were running straight for us.

"Pii!"

Filo was running circles around my head, apparently ready for a fight.

It wasn't going to be much good in a fight yet, and it would be dangerous to hang out on my head, so I stuffed the little thing into my armor.

"Pii!"

"I'm going!"

"No! Let me go first!"

"What if you get hurt, Mr. Naofumi?! Didn't you buy me so that I could fight for you?!"

"If the thing is strong enough to hurt me, just think about what it could do to you. I didn't buy you to get you hurt! It might have been different back then . . . but now you need to take care of yourself!"

"Mr. Naofumi . . ."

I turned my gaze to the monsters, the Amethyst Big Frog

and the Gray Salamander, raised my shield, and rushed them. Unfortunately my attack rating wasn't high enough to do any damage. They spit a viscous, poisonous-looking liquid at me, and I blocked it with my shield.

"Go!"

"Okay!"

She ran at them and quickly cut them with her sword. They fell easily. I wonder if her new weapon was that strong. The armor was better than I had been expecting. I had to hand it to the old guy at the weapon shop.

I butchered the monsters and let the shield absorb the parts.

The frog meat looked gross and was probably poisonous. I decided not to bother trying to sell it.

"Pii!"

Filo crawled out from my armor, walked over to the defeated monsters, and struck a defiant pose over their bodies, as if it had just killed them itself.

I wanted to ask what the thing was doing, but it was kind of cute, so I just let it go.

We walked around the area for a while longer, defeating monsters all the time. We were leveling up relatively efficiently.

By the time evening fell, I could tell that I had grown, and Filo had too. These were the results:

Naofumi: LV 23
Raphtalia: LV 27
Filo: LV 12

Filo hadn't contributed to the battles at all but had still received enough experience points to level up quickly. It looked like it had grown too.

That was good. I'd heard that young demi-humans matured along with their rising levels, so I guess it was only natural to expect monsters to level up in a similar way.

That must have been it . . .

The little chick was not so large and heavy that it was hard to hold in both hands. It was also—how to put it?—rounder. It was like a giant steamed bun. Its feathers were larger and covered its body now, and the whole guy had changed from a light pink to a darker pink.

Monster User Shield II: conditions met

Monster User Shield II: ability locked: equip bonus: monster status adjustment (small)

I hadn't noticed when Raphtalia grew before my eyes, but even I couldn't help but notice the dramatic transformation the little bird had undergone.

"Piyo."

It even chirped differently. It was heavy, so I put it down, and it walked around authoritatively.

Grumble . . .

I'd heard its stomach grumbling for a little while. Then it was louder than both me and Raphtalia. I'd made sure to buy a lot of food for it, but apparently the bird had already run out. The rancher said that they could eat anything, so I kept feeding it anything that looked like food, like piles of hay we'd found on the road. It ate all of it and still seemed hungry. That must have been proof of how quickly it was growing.

"Um . . . Mr. Naofumi?"

"I know . . . Monsters sure are amazing."

To think that it had grown this much in the course of a single day . . . It wouldn't be long before it could carry us!

It was great and something to look forward to. If it grew to be really big but was still as immature as a baby, then it could spell trouble down the line. I went to the status screen and set its settings to strict.

We went back to the inn, and I asked the innkeeper where we could keep Filo. He led us to the horse stables, which were lined with hay for Filo to make itself a bed.

"Huh? Why are the Chimera bones and meat in here?"

The meat hadn't started to rot at all, so it must have been good for keeping. Or maybe it didn't rot because the monster was from another dimension.

"We decided to hang it up here and wait for it to soften a bit. That should make further processing easier."

"Huh . . ."

But they weren't going to use it for food . . . And they wanted to process it.

"Then we will smoke it or make jerky. Once it's done, we can look for buyers. There have already been some people who stopped by and asked for some."

"Sounds good to me."

The Chimera had been very large, so they needed to use a lot of space to store the remains. It was probably the size of two full-grown cows. It probably wasn't going to make for very good food, but it seemed like there was too much there to dedicate to researchers only.

"Piyo."

Grumble . . .

Was it already hungry again? I'd bought new food on our way back to the village and had already fed it. But I guess it had already gone through our stores. Geez, where was it fitting all that food?

Pikee, Pikee, Pikee . . .

Was that its bones creaking? Was it already growing?

"I can't believe how much this grew over the day. You might be in over your head, eh?"

The innkeeper looked concerned.

"It's only at level 12."

"Huh? Level 12?"

The innkeeper shot a surprised glance at Filo.

"To grow this much in only a few days after its birth! Well, I'd swear it was at level 20! You're very impressive, Hero."

Yeah, well . . . I was using maturation adjustment, so its quick maturation was probably due to that. Every time I checked its status, the numbers were different. So I guess it really was growing very quickly.

"Piyo!"

Filo was chirping happily. It would grow up quickly.

I rubbed the bird's head until I was sure it was sleeping. Once it was snoring, Raphtalia and I went back to our room. Then I went back to studying the writing system of this world. There was so much to do. I was getting tired.

Chapter Four: Growth

The next morning, I woke up and tip-toed out of the room on my way to go see Filo so that I wouldn't wake Raphtalia, who had been up all night studying.

"Gah!"

A loud, wild voice greeted me when I entered the stables. Then I saw Filo. It had grown since the previous night. Where it had just been a round thing before, now its legs and neck had grown out. It stood there, looking something like an ostrich. It was changing so quickly! And it was growing so differently from any of the birds I knew anything about. It was now so tall that it stood up level with my chest. Still—it wasn't big enough to ride yet.

Grumble . . .

So it was already hungry again? Good thing I'd stopped off to buy some food.

If it was growing this much in a day, I don't know . . . Something about it was almost scary.

"Look at you! And you just hatched yesterday!"

"Gah!"

I found myself smiling just looking at the thing.

It wasn't like I just discovered some deep-rooted love

of animals or anything like that. I was just thrilled at the possibilities. I started thinking over all the things it could do for me once it was big enough. If it could pull a cart, I'd love to have it do so.

Its feathers had grown again and changed colors. Now they were a mix of white and very light pink.

In an effort to clean up a bit, I let the shield absorb some of the feathers.

Monster User Shield III: conditions met
Monster User Shield III: ability locked: equip bonus: maturation adjustment (medium)

Man, just imagine what I could have gotten if I'd given the shield some of its blood. I should give Raphtalia another haircut and try absorbing more of her hair.

Filo had only just been born, but here it was, running around and happy.

"Gah!"

It wasn't a dog, but I picked up a twig and threw it as far as I could for Filo to fetch. We played that way for a while.

Filo was so fast that sometimes it caught the twig before it had a chance to fall. Then it brought the twig back. It was pretty talented. Anyway, I played with Filo until Raphtalia woke up. This whole "pet" thing was kind of refreshing,

Thinking back on it, people back in my world kept dogs and cats. They were pretty cute.

A long time ago, at my school, there was a wild cat. It was really nervous around people, and everyone said that it wouldn't approach you if you didn't have food. But it approached me.

In elementary school we had a class in which we took care of animals, and everyone else complained about the chickens because they pecked. But they never pecked me. So I guess you could say that I sort of liked animals. Or at the very least, I didn't hate them.

"Mmm . . . There you are, Mr. Naofumi. And look at that smile! I don't think I've ever seen you so happy."

Raphtalia had woken up and come to find me. She entered the stables looking grumpy.

She had a twisted, tired smile on her face.

"What is it?"

"Oh, it's nothing."

"Gah!"

Filo was lightly tapping at Raphtalia with its beak.

She sighed.

"I guess there's no getting around it . . ."

Raphtalia smiled, and reached out her hands to lightly pet Filo's cheeks.

"Gah . . ."

Filo looked really happy and squinted its eyes as it saddled up next to Raphtalia and rubbed against her.

"I wonder where we should go today."

"Good question. You'd probably like to try and save on food costs for Filo, so how about we head out to the plains to the south of here?"

"Hmm . . . That's a good idea."

There were tons of different grasses growing in that area, and plenty of them could be used for medicine. Raphtalia was right . . . It would be a good place. Our immediate goal was to get the best equipment that we could, and we'd need money for that.

"Right on. Okay, let's get going."

"Gah!"

"Okay!"

So we went out to the fields and fought monsters until we leveled up.

Naofumi: LV 25
Raphtalia: LV 28
Filo: LV 15

As for the grasses, I spent most of my energy looking for things that Filo could eat, so we didn't end up actually collecting very much for medicine. I did go ahead and let the shield absorb all the things we found, but I didn't get much out of it except for a couple of small status bonuses.

And I still hadn't found a shield that would teach me intermediate compounding recipes.

That evening, Filo grew into what appeared to be a full-grown Filolial.

"Sure is growing up quick! Normally it would take them three months or more to reach this size . . ."

The innkeeper and the rancher were both surprised. They couldn't believe how fast Filo was growing.

It must have been because of the maturation adjustment, both small and medium, that I was using.

"If only I thought to absorb the ink way back when I bought Raphtalia . . ."

"Ahaha . . ."

I wondered if Raphtalia wished that she, too, could grow that quickly.

Creaaakkkkk.

I could hear the creaking and cracking of bones again. Filo must be growing.

"Gah!"

Filo was standing right in front of me and looked to be large enough to ride.

"You want to carry me around?"

"Gah!"

Filo called out and dipped its head for me to climb onto its back as though that were the most obvious answer.

"Thank you."

I didn't have reigns or a saddle, but I wondered if it would be okay. The thing was practically asking me to climb on, so I did. The shield would help me survive any falls—my defense rating was through the roof.

As for comfort . . . Well, the feathers helped with that. If I could find my balance, it wouldn't be bad at all.

I'd never ridden a horse, but I'd ridden a dog once. When I was a kid, some other kid in the neighborhood had a dog, and they let me ride it once. The owners said that they had never been able to ride it, but it wasn't any problem for me. The dog carried me around just fine.

"Gah!"

Filo quickly stood up.

"Argh!"

I was so high off the ground, and from my vantage everything looked . . . different. So this is what the world would look like from Filo's back.

"Gaaaaah!"

I thought that Filo was just calling out in happiness, but then it suddenly took off running!

"Um . . . Hey!"

"M . . . Mr. Naofumi!"

Dash! Dash! We were running!

It was so fast! I'd see something, and then it would be

behind us just as quickly. I heard Raphtalia calling for us, but she was already far in the distance.

Dash! Dash!

Filo circled the village once before returning to the stables. Then it sat down and let me off.

"Are you all right?!"

Raphtalia looked worried as she ran over to me.

"Yeah, I'm fine. Filo is so fast!"

Filo didn't look tired in the least and soon turned to preening its feathers.

Filo ran much quicker than I had been expecting. This might have been my best purchase yet.

"All right, that seems like enough for today. Let's head back to our room."

Something had a grip on my armor's collar. I turned to see Filo looking back at me.

"What is it?"

"Gaaah!"

It almost looked like it was crying. It kept balking at me.

"Huh?"

I gave up and turned to leave again, but once again it pulled at my collar.

"What is it?"

"Gaah!"

Filo's feet were digging into the ground, like it was determined to make a stand.

"What? You want to play more?" Raphtalia asked, and Filo shook its head. Could it understand what we were staying?

"Are you lonely?"

It nodded.

"Gaah!"

It opened its wings and cried out.

"But there's nothing we can . . ."

I certainly didn't want to sleep in the stables, and I don't think the innkeeper would be happy if we brought a huge monster into the room.

"Let's stay with it until it falls asleep!"

"Oh . . . Um . . . Okay."

The thing was so big, but it had only hatched two days ago. Maybe it was still a baby and just wasn't ready to be left on its own in the stables overnight. Raphtalia and I decided to do our nightly study session in the stables.

Filo sat in its nest and quietly watched us study.

Piki . . .

"Geez . . . Am I ever going to be able to read this stuff?"

"If we can't find a shield to do it, then this is our only option. Besides, if you are always depending on that Legendary Shield, well . . . it's probably not best for you."

"Raphtalia . . . You sure don't hold anything back these days."

"That's right. So let's get back to studying so that we can learn magic!"

What was so wrong with wanting things to be easier than they were? I hoped that all this work would actually amount to something. We kept on studying in the stables until we heard Filo's steady snores.

Then we went back to the room, and I tried my hand at compounding some new herbs.

I still couldn't read the recipes, so I was really just guessing.

Chapter Five: Kick and Run

The next day Raphtalia woke up with me, and we both went to the stables.

"Gahh!"

When Filo caught sight of us it called out happily and ran over to greet us.

"Are you already all grown up now?"

Filo looked to have grown another head overnight.

Already it looked to be the size of the full-grown Filolials I'd seen walking around town back at the castle.

It was now white, with only very small tints of pink in places. It was pretty.

"Are you hungry?"

"Gah?"

Filo turned its head to the side and looked confused. Good, so it was out of its growth spurt.

Piki . . .

There was that strange sound again. It was growing so fast that its body couldn't keep up.

We ate breakfast and then sat down to discuss our plans for the day.

The villagers all seemed very busy. They were bustling about making repairs.

"Gahh . . .."

There was a cart being pushed down the road, filled with materials for repairs. Filo looked at, almost longingly . . .

"You want to pull that thing?"

"Bet he does."

"What is it, Hero?"

Raphtalia and I were talking and pointing at the cart when a villager stopped by and asked.

"My Filolial was staring at that cart, so I was wondering if he wanted to pull it or something."

"Yes, Filolials are quite instinctual that way."

The villager nodded in agreement and looked over at Filo.

"Everyone is so busy with the repairs, but we still need all the help we can get. Hero, if we promised to give you a cart, do you think you could help out?"

"Mmm . . ."

It wasn't a bad idea. And since I finally had a useful monster, it only made sense to put it to work. If it all went well, we could free up our own travel time to do other things.

"What do you need from us?"

"They are cutting trees for lumber in a nearby forest. Do you think you could help carry the wood back to the village?"

"The forest . . ."

Come to think of it, I hadn't visited that forest yet.

"It might take us a little time. Is that all right?"

"Sure."

We were talking it over when I saw someone I recognized from outside of the village. They were in a group and were running over to us on a carriage pulled by a Knight Dragon.

The leader was in chainmail and wore a blinding silver breastplate. He carried a conspicuous spear.

That's right. It was Motoyasu and Bitch. They climbed down from the carriage.

"Hey! All you villagers, let's all gather around, shall we?!"

The busy villagers all set their work aside and started walking over to the intruders. Then Bitch unrolled a large sheet of parchment and started haranguing everyone.

"Citizens! In recognition for his glorious victories in the last wave of destruction, the King of these lands has granted this man, Motoyasu Kitamura, governorship over these territories."

What? Governorship? To Motoyasu?

Motoyasu, as if he could hear my thoughts, suddenly shouted.

"Which means that I, the Spear Hero, am now in control here. I've been asked to oversee the reconstruction efforts! I expect your cooperation from here on out! Make sure that you have secured proper funding for your projects before you purchase materials!"

"What?!"

The majority of the villagers looked skeptical of their new leader.

That was only natural. During the wave, when the village was under attack, what had the Spear Hero done for them? Nothing! And yet here he was, supposed to be their new leader? Of course they wouldn't accept this new appointment so easily.

Besides, being given governorship for fighting a battle? Why was the Crown so close to Motoyasu?

"You must be mistaken. You see, I am the governor here."

A man in the crowd raised his hand and addressed Motoyasu. That, too, seemed natural. Why would anyone just roll over and accept a random new appointment?

Granted, it was an official order, so I guess there wasn't much they could do by way of rebellion, but still—people were going to be aggravated.

"What are you implying? Are you going to disobey an order from your king?"

"I'm not saying that, only that it seems odd that . . ."

"Silence!"

Bitch sure seemed to think she ran the show. I really wanted to walk over and give her a hard smack across the face.

But wait . . . Did that mean that this village belonged to Motoyasu now? Dammit! That would mean that I had to move on . . . again. The innkeeper had been letting us stay for free, so I was hoping to stay based in Riyute for as long as I could.

"Ha! What's this? Why are you here, Naofumi?"

He saw me in the crowd and called out to me.

"I've based my activities here."

"Huh? You mean you're still working in a spot like this? Oh man, that's the Shield for you . . . always way behind. You must understand that this village belongs to Motoyasu now, and he will not tolerate criminals on his lands. Get on your way."

I really wanted to shut her up.

So I guess this means that Bitch was really the one in control. But what did she want? I could only imagine . . .

"First order of business: there will now be a toll levied on those entering and exiting the village. If we don't, we will never be able to raise appropriate restoration funds. The fee due upon entrance will be 50 pieces of silver, and the fee upon exit will be 50 pieces of silver. That makes for a total of one gold piece."

"But that's . . . With taxes like that, we'll never be able to survive!"

"Oh, it's not that much money."

Motoyasu clearly had a warped sense of what money was worth to these people.

A piece of gold was . . . worth a lot of money. For these people to live in relative comfort, they only needed 20 pieces of bronze a day. If you stayed in the inn, a piece of silver would get you a room and a good meal.

Their new taxes were worth 100 days of life. Who could afford to eat with a tax like that?

"What is the problem? Does anyone take issue with our edict?"

"Of course they do."

Bitch glared at me when I spoke up.

"You've just been appointed governor, and then you show up and levy a huge tax on your first visit? Think about it . . ."

"You know . . . he's kind of right, Myne. Think we could drop it to a level that the villagers can afford?" Motoyasu asked Myne.

When he did, she turned to me with demonic fury in her eyes. Just as quickly, it vanished, and she was batting her eyelashes at Motoyasu.

"If we do not learn perseverance along with our pain, the village will never recover from this calamity. The previous governor may consider himself relieved by the authority of the Crown."

"How dare you!" the governor shouted in anger.

The rest of the villagers were shouting also.

"Hey! That's not fair!"

"What are you planning on doing for us?!"

"Now, now . . . Do you know what it means to revolt against the Crown? Perhaps we will have to teach you."

Bitch raised her hand, and knights came sauntering into the village, mounted on their dragons.

Were they planning on starting a fight? Violent fools!

Motoyasu was looking at them impatiently, like he didn't like that he was being forced to stoop to this level. But he was the real criminal here.

"Hey! Now if you don't . . ."

Then Myne was suddenly surrounded by a group of men in black, like a group of ninjas.

"Hey . . ."

"Ms. Myne, yes? Surely you have been informed of our arrival. We have brought a message for you."

"What is it?"

One of the ninjas stepped forward and handed her a rolled sheet of parchment.

What? Were they assassins or something? I guess things like that existed in this world too.

Bitch stood there looking pissed off as she read from the parchment. Then all the color drained from her face.

What was it? What did it say?

"Who the hell are you?"

"We are employed by a certain someone. We have reason to believe you know of whom we speak."

"But I . . ."

Answer them. This is no time to be feigning ignorance! I was about to yell at her when . . .

"It's a battle!" Bitch exclaimed authoritatively.

"What?"

What was she even talking about? What battle? With who? Motoyasu also seemed to have no idea what was going on.

"You must race our dragons to determine the governorship of these lands."

"What the hell?"

I didn't know what was written on that parchment, but it couldn't have been something that stupid.

"If you don't, we won't relinquish control!"

After Myne shouted, the ninjas all began whispering among themselves. It sounded like they were talking about what to do once the new governor was appointed.

"Very well then. We will use the fastest monster in this village."

"No."

Myne was pointing in my direction. I was gripping Filo's reigns in my hand, and her finger moved to point at Filo.

"The Shield Hero will race for you."

"But . . ."

What sense did it make to appoint me? I wasn't even from the village.

The governor looked over at me and smiled.

"Shield Hero, won't you please come to our aid? From what I saw yesterday, your Filolial is very quick on its feet."

"No way!"

Why should I be involved in all this?

"If you win, we can promise you just compensation."

"And if I lose?"

"Nothing will happen to you . . . Besides, your Filolial looks like she wants to race, doesn't she?"

Filo was staring at the dragons and snapping her eyes from one to the next in quick succession. I had to tug on the reigns. In a sudden fury, she seemed like she might dash off to attack Motoyasu and his cohorts at any moment.

"Considering the long-held enmity between dragons and Filolials, it seems only natural that the bird is ready to race them. It should be a good match."

What a pain in the ass . . . though I suppose I didn't stand to lose anything if we failed.

"What do you think, Mr. Naofumi?"

"Hm . . ."

Well I certainly didn't want to hang out in Motoyasu's territory, and I felt like it would be a shame to leave the village so soon after I'd gotten on good terms with the inhabitants. And I'd started to get a handle on the surrounding areas too. I would have to win if I wanted to stay.

"Fine then. Let's do this."

I slowly climbed up on to Filo's back and situated myself. Then I turned to Motoyasu.

"Ahahahaha! Look at the guy on his plump chick! Bwahaha!"

His cohorts were holding their stomachs and laughing forcefully.

I had no idea what they thought was so funny, but I couldn't stand being laughed at. I felt blood rising hot up my neck.

"What the hell, Motoyasu?"

"Ha! I mean, I thought it was funny that you were walking around with that thing. And now! Now you say you're going to race on it! Ahahaha!"

"What the hell was so funny?"

Was I riding it wrong? What did they think I was doing with a Filolial anyway, if not to ride it?

"Ha! You look like a fool! First of all, dragons are way cooler than birds. Second of all, look at that thing! It's got pink all mixed up in its white feathers—obviously you bought yourself a cheap bird!"

"I don't know what color you think it should be . . ."

I still didn't get what was so funny about it.

I was trying to figure it out when Motoyasu walked over to Filo, pointing and laughing the whole time.

"Gahhh!"

Filo reared back and kicked him hard in the crotch.

I saw it. I saw his laughing face suddenly contort into an expression of confused pain. His whole body spun in drunken spirals, and he reeled back from the force of the kick.

"Ugh . . .!"

Man . . . I'd never been so happy in my whole life. I hadn't even seen it coming. Happiness visits when you least expect it.

"Kyaaaaah! Oh, Mr. Motoyasu!"

Ahaha . . . that kick must have crushed his balls.

It felt so good. That one kick was worth all the money I'd

spent on Filo so far. That's my monster. It was getting revenge for me. Filo, you'll eat good tonight—I'll see to that.

"Gaah!"

"Coward! How dare you attack Mt. Motoyasu!"

"The race hasn't started yet, and besides, if you walk up to a monster and laugh at them, what do you expect?"

"Ugh . . . you bastard."

Motoyasu tottered to his feet. His hands cradled his crotch. The sweat oozing down his face made his pain evident.

I ran my hand over Filo's head. "So are we going to start this race?"

"Of course!"

We couldn't be sure he wouldn't try something sneaky, but all we could do is stay on our toes and get it over with.

Bitch untied a dragon from the cart it had been hitched to, and Motoyasu climbed up onto its back.

"The race will consist of three laps around the village!"

The villagers ran off to draw lines in the dirt, demarcating the course.

"Good luck, Mr. Naofumi. And Filo? You take care of him, okay?"

"Sure."

"Gah!"

"I'll win. I swear it!"

The governor stood before the two of us and raised his

hands into the air. When they fell, the race would be on.

"Ready . . .. Go!"

His hands fell quickly, and we were off!

Our starting dash put us pretty much head to head.

Filo was running at a good, relaxed pace, its cadence at a steady and pleasant rhythm.

Hm? If we were comparing our speed to Motoyasu's, it seemed like Filo was faster.

This should be an easy win. We had enough of a lead that I ventured a backward glance.

"What's wrong with you?! Run faster!"

Motoyasu was desperately shouting orders at his dragon. The dragon, not wanting to lose to Filo, put in more effort and started running harder. Even still, it couldn't keep up.

Filo's specs must have been higher.

It was like a motorcycle versus a motorized bicycle. Naturally, Filo was the motorcycle in this case, whereas Motoyasu was stuck with a motorized bicycle. That's how much faster we were.

"Gaaah!"

Filo shouted in joy, as if to show off how confident we were with our lead. It was like being on a motorcycle. We cut through the wind, and the village flew by, just strips of color in my periphery. We finished the first lap, and we must have been five body-lengths or more in the lead.

"Damn!"

Bitch was cursing us in frustration.

Ahaha. It was all so easy—and it felt so good.

The villagers were gathering around the course to watch us when it happened.

"I am the source of all power. Hear my words and understand them well. I command a hole to appear before me."

"Earth Hole!"

I was watching to make sure that the castle knights didn't step into the course when a hole opened up right in front of me.

"Coward!"

The knights turned their faces away, apparently unaware of what they were being accused of.

Filo's foot clipped the side of the hole, and we went down.

"Gah?!"

"There's my chance!"

"What's your chance?! Jerk!"

Motoyasu was unperturbed by my protests, and he spurred his dragon on.

But . . .

"I am the source of all power. Hear my words and understand them well. I demand his speed be increased."

"Fast Speed!"

So someone was casting support magic on Motoyasu. And whoever had done it had also caused Filo to trip on their hidden magic hole! What was wrong with the people in this country?!

"Filo, we can't lose to people like this. Let's go!"

"Gaaaaaah!"

Filo climbed to her feet, and she chirped, as if to say that now she was serious. She took off running, faster now even than she had been before.

Before long, we were running alongside Motoyasu again.

"What?!"

Like we'd lose and let him cheat his way to victory!

Filo was running like she knew how I felt. Even though Motoyasu had been sped up, we still were able to make up the space between us by the time the second lap was over.

We were in sight of the villagers again, and I angrily thrust my finger at Motoyasu, taking care that they could all see my signal.

The villagers were pressing in to see what had changed.

"I am the source of all power. Hear my words and understand them. Slow his speed!"

"Fast Speed Down!"

"Gah?"

Filo suddenly slowed down.

"What the hell are you doing?!"

The gathered knights all turned away, as if they had no idea what I was talking about.

Motoyasu caught up with us and then passed us.

Certainly he had to know that people were going to notice. How cowardly can a guy get?!

Dammit . . . If this kept up, we would lose. I couldn't stand to think of it. There must have been something we could do!

"Gaaah!"

Filo must have been angry too. She cawed to make her dissatisfaction evident before dramatically opening her wings and leaning forward.

Hey now! She was running even faster, but it was harder to control her in the turns. When we went around a corner, she had to take the outside line.

But I still knew something about racing from games. In bike racing games, you could lean into the corners to make the bike turn quicker. I thought I should give it a try!

We came up on a corner, and I shifted my weight to help get her around it. I leaned toward the direction of the curve. It must have looked like I was hanging off of Filo's stomach.

But it worked. Filo was able to turn the corner without lowering her speed.

Yes! We were starting the third lap and we'd overtaken Motoyasu once again.

All we could do now was run to the end.

The villagers had gathered around the knights and were

watching them close to see that there were no further interruptions. That should have made victory as good as ours . . . But then the knights drew their swords, and the villagers scattered.

Everything was chaos. I could see someone among the knights beginning to chant yet another spell.

If that's how they wanted to play, I had some tricks of my own.

"Air Strike Shield!"

They had called for another hole to appear in the racing lane, but I summoned my shield to cover it.

"Go, Filo! Let's show these jerks how fast we can run!"

"Gaaah!"

Yes! Victory was as good as ours. But on our way to victory . . .

"Filo!"

"Gah!"

I spotted the knight that had been casting the spells . . . I stared him down.

"I . . . Um . . ."

From where he stood, I must have seemed like the supreme ruler of the century's end.

Filo turned her back on the cheating knight, raised her leg, and kicked him. The fool fainted on the spot.

"Gah!!"

Filo called out her victory, and we sauntered over the goal line, far in the lead and victorious.

"I . . . I lost . . ."

"It's not fair! He cheated! I demand a rematch!" shouted Bitch.

"Cheated? Who are you talking about? Who was the one casting spells?"

I pointed at the unconscious knight.

"What are you implying?"

"That guy was casting all sorts of spells to hinder our progress! That's cheating!"

"Wait . . . Was he really?"

Motoyasu chimed in, acting as if he had been unaware the whole time.

Like I'd forget that he'd shouted "Now's my chance!"

"I don't know anything about that. Even if he did cheat, what's that got to do with us? We demand justice!"

So she only wants justice when SHE loses? Ha! Give me a break.

"It didn't look that way to me."

All of the villagers nodded in agreement with the governor's announcement.

"Just as the Shield Hero was saying, there are marks on the course left by magical spells. We ran to chase off the knights, so the proof is still there."

That's right. We kicked that knight at the end so that he wouldn't be able to cover up what he had done. The villagers now surrounded him. If we just went to see the huge hole still in the racing lane, anyone would know, right off the bat, who was to blame.

"The Shield Hero planted that to make us look bad!"

"No, he did not."

What? The lady from the magic shop appeared from the crowd of villagers. Oh yeah, she had a grandchild here, she'd said.

"The Shield Hero can only use support and restorative magic. The girl with him can only use light and dark magic, and therefore neither of them could have formed these holes in the earth."

"Oh, great! The stupid magic shop lady thinks she knows everything now!"

Just as Bitch shouted, the ninjas appeared again to surround her.

"It appears obvious that the Spear Hero was the recipient of unfair support. Please come with us."

Motoyasu spoke softly and tried to calm Bitch down. "We've lost this one, and therefore, as promised, we relinquish control of this village."

"Right. So get the hell out already."

"I won't lose next time."

"You lose all the time. Coward."

"I am not a coward!"

"Spear Hero, this is no time to fight. You neither, Shield Hero."

The ninjas admonished the Motoyasu gang, and they all left together.

They left the dragon behind.

"We don't need a dragon that lost to the Shield. Leave it. "

"Kyuuuu." The dragon let out a pitiful cry and was left behind.

The poor thing. It's not like he had done anything wrong.

A group of villagers walked over and pet the dragon's head before taking its reigns in hand.

"Let's keep him in the village."

"Good idea."

The dragon walked beside the villagers, its head hung low.

"I won, so give me my prize."

"Mr. Naofumi . . . just like that?"

"This village owes you so much, Shield Hero. Had they imposed a tax the likes of what they were discussing, it would have been the end of our village. Even still, can you wait a few days? If so, we can provide you with funds as well."

"Don't you need the money to make repairs?"

"You know us well."

"What's the point in digging into your repair funds just to pay me? That's not good for anyone. No thanks, but I appreciate the offer."

The last thing I wanted was to end up indebted to anyone. Besides, it would not have helped my bruised reputation. Everyone would think I shook the village down for money.

"Then we will provide you with something very convenient indeed. Tell me, Hero, do you have any interest in traveling sales?"

"Traveling sales?"

"Yes, like when you walk from village to village, town to town, and sell wares. It appears that you are supporting yourself by selling materials and medicines. If you have any interest, we could help you with such matters."

"Huh."

Did they mean a traveling merchant of some sort? In other words, instead of selling to apothecaries, I would sell directly to customers . . .

I'd have to give it some thought. Up until now, I'd been focused on the production side of things, but if I did what they suggested, I'd get in on the sales side of things too. That should make me a good profit.

"Not to mention, Hero, that you also happen to possess a Filolial. That will get you from place to place with relative ease and speed. If you had it pull a cart, then your business would be that much easier. If you'd like, we could provide you a commercial bill of passage."

"Commercial bill of passage?"

"Yes. Normally, traveling merchants need to visit with the local governor when they first enter a village or town and pay him a certain sum to do business there. However, if you show them the commercial bill of passage, with my seal affixed, then you should not have to pay this fee. I think you would find it quite useful."

I had to think. This farming town was very close to the Melromarc Kingdom, and it was situated conveniently close to trade routes. To be the governor of such a place must have entailed a level of authority and dignity. The villagers were aware that their village was saved during the wave due to my efforts. They must have also heard about my troubled reputation and all about what the king was doing to me, using any method he could think of to suppress my freedom. They also knew that my reputation would make further business difficult for me and therefore were offering cooperation.

"I believe it will help you conduct business in spite of your unsavory reputation. We'd like to remove obstacles from your path, and we think this will make life easier for you."

They were accepting me and being kind. I felt sincere gratitude.

"Thank you. I accept your kind offer."

In truth, it really was wonderful compensation, and it should make it easier to get some decent money. They even offered to build a carriage for Filo.

Great . . . that sure beat pushing a wheelbarrow.

"Well anyway, let's get back to reconstruction, shall we?"

"Yes."

The villagers nodded along with Raphtalia. We all went back to our own projects.

"Gah!"

Filo was on top of the world, excited to have her very own carriage.

"Great. Let's head to the forest!"

"Okay!"

"Gah!"

I pointed in the direction I wanted to go, and Filo chirped in excitement and started pulling the carriage.

Rattle . . . Rattle . . .

Ahh . . . It was so peaceful, so pleasant.

Rattle, rattle, rattle! Clatter, clatter!

Filo started pulling faster and faster, and soon we were flying down the road.

"You're too fast! Slow down!"

"I don't feel so good . . ."

Raphtalia was lying down in the back of the carriage, suddenly sick. I guess she got motion sick.

"You all right?"

"Yes . . . but . . . try not to shake the carriage so much."

"I guess you get motion sick, huh?"

"I guess I do. Are you all right, Mr. Naofumi?"

"I've never gotten sick yet."

It wasn't just alcohol that didn't affect me. I'd never gotten seasick or carsick either.

Back in elementary school, we'd taken a bus to go on a field trip. I was reading some manga and light novels that I had in my backpack when the person next to me started complaining that they felt sick, and we had to switch seats. Also, I remember that whenever we went to visit my extended family, we had to take a boat. Everyone else in my family got seasick, but not me. I remember playing games on my phone the whole time.

"We'll make sure you relax. Filo and I will make sure that we get to where we are going."

"Thank you. I'll take you up on that offer . . ."

"Gaaah!"

"Could you maybe go a little slower?"

Filo just kept on running, overjoyed, as though she couldn't hear Raphtalia at all.

Afterward, Raphtalia threw up on the side of the road. By the time we made it to the forest, she was doing all she could to suppress the nausea.

"Ugh . . . Ugh . . ."

Raphtalia's pale face made me feel bad. Maybe I should have slowed the carriage down more.

"Sorry."

"Gah . . ."

Filo, too, looked downcast, as though guilty.

"I'm . . . I'm fine."

"You don't look fine. Let's find a place for you to rest."

"Why hello there, Shield Hero."

There was a small house over by the woods, and a villager who looked something like a lumberjack came out from it.

"Yeah, the villagers asked me to come pick up some wood here."

"Um . . . Is your friend there all right?"

"I think . . . I dunno. Probably not. I'd like to let her get some rest. Do you know of a good place?"

"There's a place in my house she could rest for a while."

The lumberjack led us over to his house, and I lent Raphtalia my shoulder to steady herself on the way. Once we were inside, we laid her down on the bed.

"Let's find some enemies that are easy enough for Filo to take care of in this area. Then we'll just focus on carrying the luggage."

Raphtalia apparently got motion sick rather easily, so we'd have to slow the pace down a bit.

"Do me a favor and load the carriage up with the wood, if you will. We'll be back in a little while."

"Okay."

I unhitched Filo from the carriage, and she looked at the house, then at me.

"Let's go!"

"Gah!"

Considering how badly she had hurt Motoyasu, I was expecting a pretty impressive fight with her.

We went to go walk around the forest.

Once we were under the trees for a while, I was surprised at how few monsters we encountered. Filo and I just kept on walking through the silent forest.

People always talk about how peaceful and relaxing the silence of the forests is, but I'd never understood what they meant until now.

That reminds me, ever since I'd come to this world, I don't think I'd ever had the opportunity to just walk around and enjoy the scenery.

I felt so peaceful now. It must have been the look on Motoyasu's face after he'd taken the brunt of Filo's kick.

No, that's not it.

It was because Raphtalia had believed in me.

And now she was back at that house, sick from the carriage ride.

I felt . . . lonely.

Thinking back on it all, we'd really only been together for two or three weeks. And yet it already felt so natural to be

THE RISING OF THE SHIELD HERO 2   113

together. She was just a little kid back then, and I felt like it had been forever since she'd grown into the young woman she was now.

I'd decided to try and take over the role of her parents . . . but what, exactly, was I supposed to do? And the wave was still coming.

We still had over a month until the next wave came . . . and yet . . .

"If only there was some kind of medicine for motion sickness . . ."

Chapter Six: Wings

We finished our walk in the woods. Raphtalia still wasn't feeling well, so we left her resting and made a run to the village to drop off the lumber. By the time we returned, she was feeling much better.

"How are you?"

"Better."

"That was . . . fast!"

The lumberjack was shocked at how quickly we were able to get to the village and back.

"This one is pretty quick on its feet," I answered and ran my hand over Filo's head.

"Gah!"

Filo gave an excited chirp. It's true. She really was fast.

"So should we make a real try at this forest?"

"Yes."

"Take it slow on the way back, okay, Filo?"

"Gah!"

Piki . . .

What was that sound? I thought it was a bone growing, and yet, here she was, making those weird sounds again. I hope she wasn't sick or anything like that.

We did pretty well for ourselves that day. Raphtalia was fighting at the top of her game, but I was surprised at how quick and strong Filo was turning out to be. Honestly, if you were only looking at speed and the strength of a single attack, she probably could have beat Raphtalia.

And yet, Raphtalia was apparently eager to lead the attack.

Naofumi: LV 26
Raphtalia: LV 29
Filo: LV 19

White Usapil Shield: conditions met
Dark Porcupine Shield: conditions met
Usapil Bone Shield: conditions met
Porcupine Bone Shield: conditions met

White Usapil Shield: ability locked: equip bonus: defense 2

Dark Porcupine Shield: ability locked: equip bonus: agility 12

Usapil Bone Shield: ability locked: equip bonus: stamina up (small)

Porcupine Bone Shield: ability locked: equip bonus: SP up (small)

All the abilities I'd managed to unlock were status boosts.

If there was a more efficient place to level, I could have used a better, more functional shield. But I didn't know anywhere that would be good for efficient leveling. So all I could do was work in this area to unlock the abilities and boost the stats of the shields I already had.

How many abilities had I unlocked at that point? There were so many it was hard to tell. Even still, I hadn't used any of the lower-level shields, like the Orange Small Shield, since I'd unlocked them. The most useful had probably been the Sharpening Shield, as at least its skill came in handy from time to time.

Anyway, as for the four shields I got today, I was pretty sure that I wouldn't use them once I unlocked their abilities.

When the sun started to go down, we all walked back to Riyute, and I made sure that Filo kept to a leisurely pace.

We'd have to find some way to get Raphtalia used to riding in a carriage. On our way home she had to stop and rest in the trees more than once. That slowed us down even more, and by the time we made it back to Riyute, it was already dark.

"I'm very sorry about this."

"Don't worry about it. You'll get used to it eventually."

I never got sick. I was starting to think it a little strange. I'd heard that people could get used to riding on things that used to make them sick though, so I was hoping that Raphtalia would get over her sickness relatively quickly. Granted, Filo had a tendency to run off at breakneck speed—and that wasn't helping.

"Gah!"

A transformation had already started in Filo. Honestly, it had probably started a long time ago, and we just hadn't noticed it. Or perhaps we had noticed it but had ignored it.

The next morning I noticed the transformation, and so had Raphtalia. We were both deep in thought.

"Gaah!"

When we went to the stables to check on Filo, the transformation was already complete.

Filo was . . . really, no matter how you looked at it, much bigger than any Filolial I'd seen before.

The average height for Filolials evened out somewhere around two meters and thirty centimeters. They were a lot like ostriches. But Filo was much stockier, and her neck and head were much larger.

And she stood at two meters and eighty centimeters.

When she stood up, her head hit the ceiling of the stables.

"Did I really buy a Filolial egg? I'm starting to wonder if we didn't end up with something else altogether."

"Yeah . . . I'm starting to think the same thing."

"Gah!"

Filo swallowed something that she'd been chewing on. I looked around and realized that the Chimera meat was all gone. There'd been like two whole cows' worth of meat, and now it had all vanished without a trace.

Had Filo just finished it off?

"And here I was thinking that his appetite had died off . . ."

"She's been eating it the whole time!"

"Gah!"

"Ahahahaha!"

"This is not a laughing matter!"

All right . . . what should we do? For now, at least, we could just pretend that she was a bigger Filolial than average.

Piki . . .

There was that weird sound again.

"Did you hear that?!"

"Mr. Naofumi? Could it be that your shield skills have helped her grow this much?"

"It could be. Sure. I did get a maturation adjustment (medium) bonus from that Monster User Shield III."

"Mr. Naofumi . . . You have a Slave User Shield too, don't you?"

"Yeah. It has a similar maturation bonus on it too."

"You mean . . . It works on me?"

"Yeah, I unlocked it a long time ago. I can tell it's having an effect on you."

"Noooo!"

Raphtalia screamed and ran from the stables.

"Ra . . . Raphtalia?!"

"I . . . I'd been thinking that I felt lighter on my feet more than normal these days. That was you? It's because of you!"

"Hey, calm down!"

"Am I going to get as big as Filo? I don't want to! I'm scared!"

"You're not making those weird sounds!"

"You . . . You're right. Whew! Good thing! I was so scared."

Still, I really couldn't predict what the skill would do to her.

I pictured Raphtalia bulking up and growing huge, and I looked over at Filo.

"What are you thinking about?"

"I wonder what's going on."

I ignored Raphtalia's hysterical question and moved the conversation forward.

"Maybe we should go back to the slave trader and see if he can tell us anything."

"Good idea."

There was no getting around it. I really didn't want to leave and go all the way back to Castle Town, but that seemed to be our only option.

"Gah!"

We boarded the carriage and made way for Castle Town,

but I worried about Raphtalia the whole time. I didn't want her getting sick again. On the way we fought a few monsters and stopped to feed Filo when she protested of hunger. When we finally made it to Castle Town, it was just past noon.

"Hey . . ."

I realized that Filo had changed even more. Her legs were shrinking, until she looked like some giant penguin or owl.

Still, she happily pulled the carriage, as if it were her favorite thing in the world.

But she wasn't able to pull it in the same way she had before. Before, the carriage had been tied to the reigns around Filo's body. But now Filo held the straps in little wings that she could manipulate like hands. She pulled the cart with skill.

"Gweh!"

Even her voice was different. Filo was white all over now.

"Huh?"

I climbed down from the carriage and slowly looked Filo over.

Has she . . . shrunk?

She seemed to be standing at two meters and thirty centimeters now. But her whole body seemed stockier now, like she'd made up for her lost height by expanding horizontally. She made for an imposing presence. She was like . . . one of those comically fat mascots you see around theme parks.

"Gweh?"

"It's nothing."

Was Filo aware of the changes she was going through? It was already hard to tell what kind of monster she was supposed to be.

"Yes, well . . . I don't know what to tell you. All I can do is express my own shock. Yes sir."

The slave trader was mopping the cold sweat from his face as he looked Filo over.

"Gweh?"

Filo was fatter in all directions now. It stood somehow like a mix between a human and an ostrich.

"Okay, so tell me the truth. This thing hatched from the egg we bought from you. What kind of egg was that?"

I stepped closer and leaned in as I asked. I snapped my fingers and Filo readied herself to attack if necessary.

"Gweeeeeeh!"

The slave trader, visibly flustered, flipped through sheet after sheet of documents.

"This is . . . strange. According to my records, the egg that I sold you was most definitely a Filolial egg."

"THIS is a Filolial?"

"Gweeh!"

I threw a big piece of food over to her, and she skillfully snapped it out of the air.

"Well . . . now . . ."

That reminded me . . . I don't think I'd heard any of those weird sounds from Filo for a little while now.

Did that mean that she had finally fully matured?

"And to think that this creature hatched only a few days ago. She's grown so fast! I take my hat off to you, Hero."

"Stop beating around the bush. Tell me the truth. What kind of egg did you sell me?"

"Well . . . Was this creature always the way she appears now?"

"No."

I gave him a quick summary of the maturation process we'd observed for the last few days.

"So you mean that the creature seemed to be a normal Filolial for a long time?"

"Yes, only now it's like she's become something completely different."

"Gweh?"

Filo turned her head to the side and struck a pose. It was cute, but I think she might have been a little irritated.

Just whose fault was it that we were here though? Hm?

"Gweh."

She walked over and rubbed her whole body against mine. Then she opened her wings and hugged me close. It only made sense, since she was a bird, that she'd be warm. But her high body heat was honestly almost sweltering.

"Um . . ."

Raphtalia knit her eyebrows before leaning in and grabbing my hand.

"Gweh?"

Raphtalia and Filo were now staring at one another.

"Hey, what's with you two?"

"Oh, nothing."

"Gweh, gweh."

Both of them shook their heads to the side. What was going on?

"So what is it?"

"Yes, well . . ."

The slave trader seemed at a loss for words.

Could it be that he didn't understand how to raise the very monsters that he was selling?

"I need to do some research. May I ask you to leave the monster with me?"

"If you hurt her during this 'research' of yours, I'll see to it that you pay."

"Gweh?!"

"I understand, but I will need some time. Yes sir."

"Fine. I'll leave it up to you. If anything happens, I'll hold you liable."

"Gweeeh?!"

As if she was dissatisfied with my answer, Filo flapped her

wings angrily. But a servant appeared, clipped a collar around her neck, and led her to a cage. Oddly enough, she didn't put up a fight at all. Maybe she didn't because she could see us there with her.

"All right, we'll be back tomorrow to pick her up. I sure hope you have an answer for us by then."

I made my point bluntly, and then Raphtalia and I exited the tent.

"Gweeeh!"

Even after we'd left the tent and were walking down the street, we could still hear Filo's sharp cries.

That evening, we were settling into our room in the inn when the innkeeper called for us.

"Excuse me, Hero?"

"Hm? What is it?"

"There is someone here to see you."

Who could it be? I didn't have time to ask, as the innkeeper told me the person was waiting for us at the counter. I looked around him to see, and sure enough, there was a man I'd never seen waiting there.

"What do you want?"

"I am, um . . . I am a monster trainer . . ."

A monster trainer? Ah, a slave trader. Of course he wouldn't want to introduce himself that way here, in front of everyone.

"What is it?"

"Um . . . We would like to return the monster you have left with us, so I've come to meet you."

"What?!"

It had only been a couple of hours since we'd left the tent. What could have happened?

Raphtalia and I made our way to the tent as quickly as we could, and as soon as we were within earshot, we could here Filo's cries.

"Oh, hello there. You'll have to pardon me for calling at such an hour as this. Yes sir."

The slave trader came to meet us at the door. He looked exhausted.

"What is it? I thought we agreed that you'd take her for the night?"

"That was what I'd intended. But your monster has caused us a fair bit of trouble you see . . ."

"Gweeeeeeeh!"

Filo was rocking the cage, but once she caught sight of us she calmed down a bit.

"Your monster has broken three cages and sent five of my servants to the hospital with heavy injuries. Three of our other monsters have also sustained heavy injuries. Yes sir."

"I'm not going to pay you for your troubles."

"Always thinking of money, even at a time like this. I take

my hat off to you, Hero. Yes sir."

"Anyway, what is it? Did you figure out the problem?"

"No . . . However, I have heard an eyewitness report of something called the Filolial Master."

"Master?"

"Specifically, it refers to a Filolial that has taken on leader status of a large Filolial flock. It's a rather famous story among adventurers."

Apparently the slave trader had thrown his net pretty wide when he tried to figure out what the issue with Filo was.

Wild Filolials formed large flocks and apparently they were controlled by a leader.

This master would only appear before human eyes very rarely. Was he suggesting that this "King of the Filolials" was Filo?

"Huh . . ."

Guess it was some kind of folklore.

I could have let the monster out and absorbed it into my shield. Then I would know for sure, but it would also kill Filo. I could butcher it and absorb the blood and wings and stuff, but since she was my monster, that would only unlock the Monster User Shield. There was something else I could unlock, but I wasn't a high enough level, and my skill tree hadn't progressed enough.

"Gweh?"

If the monster was on your side, its information wasn't displayed on the status screen, except for deeming it an ally. Now, if the monster was an enemy, I could have seen its name.

"So what do you call this master thing?"

"Filolial King or Filolial Queen."

"Filo's a girl, so she must be a queen."

"Yes. And she's taken a liking to you, and besides, I couldn't sell her like this if I tried."

"Sir . . ."

"Huh? Did you hear that?"

"Hear what? I didn't hear anything."

"Um . . . I . . ."

Raphtalia covered her mouth and was pointing at Filo's cage. The slave trader's assistant was also pointing breathlessly. The slave trader and I followed their gaze to try and see what everyone was so excited about.

"M . . . Master!"

There was a naked girl with wings there in the cage, bathed in the afterglow of a radiant white light.

Chapter Seven: Transformation

"Hey! Open up in there!"

I was banging on the door to the weapon shop, which had already closed for the day. Eventually the owner slowly opened the door, looking groggy and upset.

"What is it there, Little Hero? I've been closed for hours."

"We don't have time for that!"

I'd covered Filo with my cape, and I pushed her forward so the owner could see her.

"Little Hero Boy, don't come bragging to me about your new slaves."

"That's not it at all!"

What kind of person did he think I was? If I met the guy he seemed to think I was, I'd punch him in the face.

"Master? What's wrong?"

"You shut up."

"I don't wanna!"

What the hell was going on?

Everything went crazy after that. The slave trader kept thrusting his finger at me. His assistant was speechless. Raphtalia too. As for Filo, she wanted to get closer to me, so she became a girl, and before I knew it I'd taken her with me and was banging on the door of the weapon shop.

Tear! Riiiiiip!

She transformed before our eyes, and the cape was torn to tatters.

She'd turned into the Filolial Queen (tentative name).

That damn bird! You know that cape isn't free?

"Wh . . ."

The owner was at a loss for words. He looked up at the giant bird. Filo suddenly turned back into a little girl and held my hand. The cape fluttered down from above and covered her head.

"See what I mean?"

"Oh . . . Yeah."

The guy twisted his face in confusion and led us inside.

"So why did you come here? You want equipment for her?"

"Are there any clothes that could survive this transformation? Or hey—why is she transforming in the first place?!"

"C'mon, kid. Settle down."

That's right. Why was this happening? Why was Filo suddenly a little girl?

There were small wings on her back, left over from the transformation probably, and she had blue eyes. She looked like a little angel. And her face was so little and cute—she looked like a drawing. She looked to be around 10 years old. She was a bit smaller than Raphtalia had been when we'd first teamed up.

GRUMBLE . . . A classic sound of hunger came rumbling from Filo's new human stomach.

"Master! I'm hungry!"

"You'll have to wait."

"I don't wanna!"

"All right then, you can have some of my dinner."

The shop owner went to a back room and came back with a pot of soup.

"Now you'll have to . . ."

"Yay! Yummy!"

She snatched the pot from him and poured the contents down her throat in one quick movement.

"Hm . . . Well, it wasn't the most delicious soup ever . . ."

She handed the pot back to him, and he accepted it in silence and then shot me a glance.

"Sorry about that."

"Hey, kid, you better buy me some dinner someday."

She was already costing me a fortune!

"But now that you mention it, I do think I had some clothes for demi-humans that were capable of transforming. Which reminds me; go to a normal clothes store if you want clothes."

"You want me to barge into a store I don't know with a naked girl at this time of night? One that turns into a monster?"

"You got a point there. Anyway, hold on."

He went into the back of the shop and I could hear him shuffling various boxes around.

"I don't know if these will fit, and they are seasonal clothes anyway—so don't get your hopes up."

"Fine."

It took him quite a while of hunting back there before he eventually returned.

"Sorry, but I don't think I have anything big enough to survive the transformation."

"What?!"

But that was my only idea . . . No, I . . . What should I do? There was this little naked girl hanging off of my arm, and I couldn't find any clothes to put on her. I was finally starting to repair my horrible reputation, and now this! This wouldn't help one bit.

"Master!"

"Don't you dare transform!"

Even if I could set certain rules for the monsters I controlled, there was no setting to prevent the monster from turning into a human. Monsters turning into humans! It must have been rare.

"But I wanna . . .!"

What would satisfy this girl?!

She refused pretty much everything I said. Was she in a rebellious phase? She'd only been born a few days earlier, so that didn't seem very likely.

"Because if I stay the way I normally am, you won't sleep with me, will you, Master?"

She squeezed my hand hard and smiled, looking up at me with beaming eyes.

"What? I have to sleep with you now?"

"I'm lonely . . ."

"Oh boy . . . You're in for it now, Hero Boy."

I wasn't summoned to this world so that I could babysit. Even still, I guess I had decided to watch out for Raphtalia.

"That reminds me. Where's Raphtalia?"

"I finally caught up."

The door swung open and Raphtalia came in, nearly out of breath.

"You ran off so quickly . . . I've been looking for you."

"Sorry about that."

"Yay! Raphtalia!"

Filo waved excitedly to Raphtalia.

"I'm not giving Master back!"

"What is this kid saying?"

"You won't give me back? You know I'm not yours!"

"Because Master is my papa!"

"No, I'm not. I'm your . . . owner."

"You're not. Then what about Raphtalia?"

"Raphtalia is like my daughter."

"That's not true!"

"Huh? I don't follow . . ."

"Anyway, I don't have the clothes you wanted. I'll look around for you, but you should go home for now."

"Right . . . Sorry."

"Thanks for the soup!"

"I swear, kid . . . You're always showing up and surprising me."

We left the shop and made our way back to the inn, but once we were on our way, Raphtalia stopped.

"Um . . . the slave . . . I mean monster trainer was looking for you."

"Huh? Oh. Okay."

We changed course and returned to the tent, where the slave trader was waiting for us.

"Well that was certainly unexpected. Yes sir."

"Sure was."

He pointed over at Filo, who was wrapped in the cape.

"Filolial Queens are capable of very advanced feats of transformation. I think they do this so that they may hide out among the other Filolials without interference from humans."

I get it now. So these kings and queens were able to change how they looked to hide out among the other Filolials. Filo used that ability to turn into a human.

"I am very surprised and excited to have the opportunity to see and study one of these. They are very rare, you know. Your ability with monster training must be very impressive. Yes sir."

"Huh?"

"That you could raise a Filolial so well, and so quickly, that it became a queen is very impressive. How were you able to do it?"

There we go. Now I knew what the slave trader wanted. If he could figure out how to produce more of these kings and queens, especially considering their rare transformation abilities, he'd be able to sell them for a massive profit.

"I think it has something to do with my Legendary Shield."

I really did think that Filo's amazing maturation had something to do with the maturation adjustment ability the shield had given me. Or at least I didn't have any other ideas.

"I was afraid you'd respond with some equivocation like that. How much money would it take to get you to tell me?"

"It's not like that!"

"Then I will provide you with another Filolial hatchling, and you can raise it . . ."

"No thanks!"

I would not be able to afford raising another one. And besides, I needed to think about getting Filo some clothes. The last thing I needed was another mouth to feed.

"I guess the only other thing that might have done it, you know . . . that thing . . ."

"What thing, exactly?!"

Ew, the slave trader was excited, and his eyes were shining. Gross.

It was just something I'd thought of, but Filo did eat the Chimera meat. That's not to say that it caused her to transform, but it was true.

"Well then, that's a shame."

The slave trader sighed and stepped back, either from disappointment or simply because he didn't believe me.

"I can supply you with another Filolial at any time, so don't hesitate to stop by. Yes sir."

"I'd like to refuse . . ."

"If you raise it into something useful, I'll see to it that you are properly compensated."

"Ha! I'll think about it when I have a bit more time and money on my hands."

I was aware that I was becoming a bit of a miser, but this conversation only set my mind further. Now being frugal was a conviction.

"Speaking of which, what should we do?"

"About what?" Filo stuck her head into the conversation and asked.

"About YOUR condition."

"I'm sleeping with Master!"

"I won't let you!"

"Aw, but I want to! Raphtalia wants to keep Master all to herself!"

"I do NOT!"

What were these girls fighting over?

"Okay, Filo. Let's sleep in the stable attached to the inn, okay?"

"No way!"

She snapped out a refusal. The way she did it was very bird-like.

"I'm sleeping with you, Master!"

It was just like a kid. Kids always wanted to sleep with their parents.

"Okay, okay."

"Mr. Naofumi?!"

"If we keep saying no she's just going to whine the whole time. I guess we need to bend a little too."

"I suppose you are right."

Raphtalia whispered her agreement, very disappointed.

"But you can't walk around naked in front of people anymore."

"Okay!"

Did she really understand? Whatever. All I could do is pray that the owner of the weapon shop would think of something in time.

We went back to the inn, paid the innkeeper for an extra person, and went up to our room. Our typical evening activities of studying and compounding were no longer possible now that Filo was running around.

"Wow! The bed is so soft!"

Filo was jumping up and down on the bed. It took a while to calm her down, and by then we were all tired enough to fall asleep.

Why is it so hot?!

"Ugh . . ."

My body wouldn't move the way I wanted it to. What was going on?

I slowly opened my eyes to find myself surrounded by white. I was covered in feathers.

Snore . . . Snore . . .

The whole bed was snoring!

I finally raised my face from the feathers to find that I wasn't sleeping on the bed anymore but on Filo's massive stomach, as she had returned to her Filolial form in the night.

Apparently she had rolled from the bed and hugged me against her, using me as a pillow as she slept.

"Get up, you fat chicken!"

Who gave her permission to turn back into a bird?

Yawwwwn.

Oh? So she could talk, even though she was a bird now?

"What . . . What are you doing?!"

Raphtalia was rubbing her eyes. Then, when she saw us, she screamed and pointed her finger at us.

"Raphtalia! Help me!"

I was hitting Filo, but she never woke up. It was probably because my attack power was so low though.

"Filo! Wake up!"

"Mmmm . . . Oh! Master!"

Filo rolled off me.

I could hear the floorboards creaking under the burden. Surely there was only so much weight that they could bear.

"Wake up!"

It didn't look like she was going to let me go and wake up anytime soon.

"Wake up!"

Raphtalia ran over and pried Filo's wings apart, creating just a big enough space for me to slip out.

"This is pretty intense for a morning."

"Hrm?"

Filo was suddenly noticing my absence, and as she started to look for me she finally came to her senses. She noticed that Raphtalia and I were shooting daggers at her, and she looked confused as to why.

"What happened?"

"First things first, turn back into a human!"

"Huh? But I just woke uuuuup . . ."

Dammit! I didn't want to do it this way, but I didn't have any other choice.

I opened up my status screen, looked at Filo's settings, and checked the box that demanded she do as I say. Now she had no choice but to do as I say.

"Turn back into a human!"

I turned to Filo and shouted the order.

"But I . . . I want to sleep with Master a little bit more!"

But the mark of the monster trainer curse appeared on her chest and started to glow.

"Huh?"

"If you don't listen, it will hurt you."

The glowing curse seal grew to cover her whole chest, then continued to expand.

Yaaaawn!

Glowing geometric patterns appeared on her wings and began to fly toward the glowing pattern on her chest.

They collided, and with a small fizzle, the monster trainer seal faded away.

"Huh?"

I quickly reopened the status screen only to find that the boxes I'd previously checked had all been unchecked. I tried to check them again, but no matter how many times I attempted it, the boxes remained empty. What's the use of a monster that doesn't follow orders?

Dammit! The whole reason I bought a monster in the first place was so it would do what I said!

That damn slave trader. Just you wait. I'm coming to see you . . . You better be waiting!

Chapter Eight: Carrot and Stick

"Slave Trader!"

First thing in the morning, we set out for the slave trader's tent.

"What is wrong, Hero? This early in the morning? Yes sir."

"The monster seal you put on my Filolial didn't work. It was junk. Depending how you respond to my complaints, my monster and slave might make a real mess of your place here. Right?"

"I'm hungry, so I'll be back later."

"If you don't behave yourself, we'll make breakfast out of YOU."

"The seal we'd put on Filo wasn't working, and I couldn't even take it off."

"You don't say? Tell me more about it."

I explained the morning's events to the slave trader. It was pretty hard going from that point on. Eventually I calmed Filo down and convinced her to return to human form, and then we all made our way to the tent. Raphtalia was clearly on edge, worrying the whole time about keeping Filo from doing anything crazy.

"It seems that a normal monster seal is not strong enough

to control a Filolial Queen. Yes sir."

"What does that mean?"

"Very powerful monsters cannot always be restrained by a normal monster seal. The Knight Dragons, for example, require a special seal."

"So a normal seal isn't enough to control Filo?"

"That right."

The slave trader opened a notebook and began frantically scribbling in it like he couldn't stand to let these new developments go unrecorded.

"So are you going to put on a special seal for me or what?"

"Unfortunately we don't offer that service for free here."

"What?"

"Well it does cost a fair amount of money to perform; therefore, we are unable to offer it without compensation. There is only so much we can do. Yes sir."

So I guess he wouldn't do it for free.

"How much?"

"With how much I believe I can expect from you in the future, Hero, I'll give you a deal at only 200 pieces of silver."

Ugh . . . That was expensive.

"Isn't there anything . . ."

"Before you continue, I'll have you know that the typical market price is 800 pieces of silver. I have great respect for you, Hero, and therefore would never lie to you."

Ugh! That hit where it hurt.

I recovered from the shock and, my mind still reeling and with extreme trepidation, handed the slave trader 200 pieces of silver.

"If you're lying, I'll let my friends here rip you apart."

"Naturally. Yes sir."

All of a sudden I noticed that Filo had returned to her Filolial Queen form. Raphtalia was holding onto one of the wings, as if it was her hand, and led Filo into the room.

"Just stay still for a minute, okay, Filo?"

"Why?"

"If you stay still, I'll give you a present later."

"Really?"

"Really."

Filo looked thrilled, and she went to where the slave trader was pointing and stood there silently.

Good, if there was any time for magic, this was it. I caught the slave trader's eye and signaled that he should start, and he quickly nodded. Suddenly twelve robed men appeared and formed a circle around Filo. They then emptied a jug of some type of medicine over the floor and then turned to Filo and began chanting. The floor began to glow, and a magical square appeared.

"Wh . . . What?!"

Filo snapped her beak rapidly in protest, but she was unable to fight it off, and the square expanded to cover her.

"Ow! Ouch! Stop it!"

The monster control spell was hurting her, apparently, and she ran in distressed circles, snapping her beak here and there. The magic square began to shake.

The robed men all let out a gasp of astonishment.

"We've taken all precautions, using as many people as we have. I've never seen a monster be able to move under so much force. Who knows what she is capable of. Yes sir."

That reminds me. She was only at level 19. Just imagine how powerful she would be at 70 or something like that. The slave trader's words carried great weight.

Finally the spell subsided, the monster control spell was etched into her chest, and she quieted down.

"It is finished. Yes sir."

I could see a monster icon flashing in my periphery, but it looked different than it had before, as if to imply a greater level of control. I didn't even stop to think but quickly checked the box that detailed necessary conformity to my orders.

Huff . . . Huff . . .

Filo was nearly out of breath when she walked over to me.

"Master! That really hurt!"

I felt a little guilty about testing it so quickly, but I immediately gave her an order.

"Turn into a human."

"But it hurt so I don't wanna! Give me something yummy!"

She had immediately refused my order and demanded food, and so the curse on her chest began to shine.

"What? No! I don't like this! Make it stop!"

Filo released some type of magic that moved toward the curse, but this time it was unable to break it, and the curse itself began to react.

"Ouch! Ouch!"

Filo fell to the floor in pain.

"If you don't do as I say, it will only hurt worse."

"Ouch! Owwwww!"

She complained the whole time but finally turned into a human. Once she did, the curse stopped glowing and disappeared.

"Heh! At least it worked this time. Nice job, Slave Trader."

"Yes, well, it is very powerful magic. It's not so easy to break, you see. Yes sir."

I went to stand before Filo, who was lying on the ground.

"It cost me 100 pieces of silver to buy you, and now it's cost me 200 pieces of silver to control you. That makes for 300 pieces of silver. I'm sure you'll pay me back."

"But . . . Master!"

She was reaching out her hand for me. Talking to a little kid like this felt bad. Even still, I couldn't keep going on if my party wouldn't listen to what I told them to do.

"Do what I say."

"No!"

"Fine then. You don't want to listen to me? I'll just give you to that creepy old man over there. You want that?"

" . . .?!"

Filo finally seemed to understand her place and stopped protesting. Her face twisted up with emotion.

The slave trader was looking me over. He looked somewhat distressed but also very happy.

"How much would you buy her for?"

"Good question. She's very rare, but considering how much trouble she seems to be, I think that 30 gold pieces seems fair. Now that she has the stronger curse on her, she should be much easier to control, and there is certainly no shortage of work that I could have her do. Yes sir."

That slave-trading bastard. After all he said about not wanting her and not being able to sell her—and here he was, already with a price in mind! I didn't know what he was really up to, but I got the impression that if I gave him Filo, that would be the end of her, then and there.

And Filo, she was looking up at me, abject terror in her eyes.

This wasn't good. I'd thought that all the goodness in my heart was gone, and yet here it was, threatening to resurrect. Whether it actually came back or not would depend on Filo's behavior.

I wasn't her lovable older brother—and I wasn't the type to sit around doting on a pet.

"There you have it. If you throw another fit, I'm not going to come running, you hear? I'll give you a bitter, gross medicine that'll run through all your veins and kill you."

"No! Noooooo!"

Filo was practically screaming.

"Master! Don't hate me! Don't hate me!"

She crawled over to me and held onto my legs as she shouted.

Ugh! This was miserable . . .

"If you listen to what I say, I won't hate you. You have to listen to me."

"O . . . Okay!"

"Okay, good. So when we are sleeping in the inn, you can't turn back into a bird. You have to promise."

"Okay!"

She looked up at me, her face beaming. This was taking a real toll on my conscience.

But then I turned my eyes away from her pleading face, and the slave trader noticed and leaned in to watch, with excitement, how the scene developed.

"This play of heretical anger is astonishing, yes. I take my hat off to you again. You truly are the Legendary Shield Hero."

I didn't appreciate the aspects of my character he had

chosen to congratulate me on, but I suppose it was nothing to complain about.

"Mr. Naofumi . . . don't you think that it's enough?"

"If I don't, she won't listen to what I say. You were the same way, remember?"

Raphtalia nodded.

"You're right. It was like that."

"There are times to let someone have their way and times when you have to reel them in."

I didn't mention that I considered myself the judge of such matters.

"Ah yes, carrots and sticks! Carrots and sticks! Yes sir."

"I wasn't talking to you, Slave Trader."

And I wished he wasn't so presumptive.

"Sorry for all the trouble."

"If that's how you feel about it, then to make things easier in the future, you should teach me how you raised this Fil . . ."

"Anyway, we have somewhere to be today, so we'll just be off."

"Ah, yes. I am once again impressed that you don't allow yourself to become subject to my own pace . . . Yes, your will is very impressive indeed, Hero. Yes sir."

So that was the end of our talks for the day, and we exited the tent.

Chapter Nine: Rewards

I threw my cape around Filo, and we went to the weapon shop.

"Ah yes, our Little Hero!"

The owner threw his hand in the air at my approach, like he had been waiting for us to stop by.

"Did you find anything?"

"Yup. You just wait a minute."

He jogged to the door and put up a closed sign before motioning for us to come outside. He led us down the street to the magic shop we had visited a few days earlier.

"Now, now."

When the owner of the weapon shop poked his head in, the lady at the magic shop could not suppress a smile, and she ran to the door to meet him.

"Would you all come to the back of my shop for a moment?"

"Filo, don't turn into a bird without my permission, okay?"

"Okay . . ."

We went into the back room, which smelled very much like someone had been living there. There was a large workspace laid out.

Apparently that was where she made her spells.

The ceiling must have been about three meters tall. There was a magic square on the ground and some crystals placed delicately in the center of the room.

"Sorry about the clutter. I was just in the middle of some work."

"No problem at all. But do you sell clothes here for this girl?"

"I asked around this morning, and I heard that the lady at this magic shop knew what to do."

"Oh yes, I do."

The lady took the crystals from their place on the table, and in their place sat a large machine that looked something like an antique sewing machine.

Was it a spindle, like the thing that Sleeping Beauty pricked her finger on?

"Is that little girl really a monster?"

"Yes. So when she transforms back into her original form, her clothes rip. Filo, turn back."

I figured it was safe for her to do it here.

"Okay."

She nodded, removed the cape, and transformed back into a Filolial.

"Ah yes, now I see. This is the little Filolial you had with you the last time we spoke, is it not?"

The magic shop lady looked up at Filo, as a Filolial Queen, and asked in shocked tones.

"Does this work?"

Filo's voice was still the same as it was when she was a little girl, so it sounded very strange coming from her giant, Filolial body. Granted, I supposed it was an accepted fantasy trope that you could hold conversations with animals like this.

I looked over at Raphtalia.

"What is it?"

"Nothing."

That reminded me: Raphtalia was a demi-human. Back when I was still bright-eyed and optimistic about this world, it would have been so exciting to have her as my partner. Thinking of it that way, I could understand the way that Motoyasu had responded to seeing her back when we dueled.

Of course, that was all in the past for me.

"So shall I make some clothes for her?"

"You can make them? Clothes that won't rip when she transforms?"

"Yes, I can . . . Though if we are honest, I don't know if they qualify as 'clothes.'"

"What do you mean?"

"How do I appear to you, Mr. Hero?"

"A magic shop . . . I don't know . . . a witch?"

"That's right. So I do know something about transformation."

It wasn't like I was starting to understand anything about this world, and I couldn't be sure if I was even right. But in the manga and games that I have played and read I think I'd come across witches that could turn into animals.

"Having said that, turning into an animal is really more trouble than it is worth, considering the level of magic required and the risk involved. Still, I do from time to time. Trying to find new clothes every time you change is really a bother, you know?"

Okay, so it sounded like witches and wizards were able to transform if they wanted to.

The witch was fingering some wooden sewing tools when she answered.

"It's fine if you are back at your own house or something. But to transform in a place you aren't secure, it can be a real disaster."

"I would think so."

The main issue seemed to be clothes. You couldn't just go walking around naked.

"So there are very useful clothes that people wear when they transform. Clothes that survive the transformation and will still be there, no matter the form you take."

"I see."

"There are some famous examples among wizards and witches, even among the demi-humans. An example you might know of is the capes that vampires wear."

Yeah . . . come to think of it, I'd seen that in an old movie. They could turn into bats and wolves and things like that. I guess they existed in this world too.

"This machine here is designed to produce the thread that we make those clothes from."

"You don't say . . . but how does it work? How does the clothing survive the transformation?"

"The power that makes it look like clothing is very exact."

Her answer confused me.

"This machine turns magical power into thread. The user can decide on their own timing to turn the thread back into magic, and vice-versa."

"So you're saying that when she turns into a human, she can turn her magic power into clothing?"

"Yes, that's how it works."

She was right . . . It wasn't exactly clothing in the way I understood clothing. When Filo wasn't a human, it would turn into a magical power that dwelt within her body. Then when she turned into a girl, it would materialize as clothing.

"Okay then. Now, Filo, will you slowly turn that handle for me?"

Filo got a hold on the handle and began to turn it. When she did, a thin thread began to come out of one end of the machine. The old lady took it, wrapped it on a dowel, and started spinning the dowel to collect the thread.

"What's happening? I feel like I'm losing my energy!"

"We are turning some of your magical powers into thread, dear. You'll feel a little tired. But keep on turning that handle. We don't have enough yet to make you any clothes."

"Ugh . . . But this isn't fun!"

I guess she really was just a kid. She'd only been alive for a week, come to think of it.

Filo kept slowly turning the handle and looking absent-mindedly around the room.

When she was doing so, the jewel that was on top of the machine suddenly broke.

"Oh no. My jewel broke! Without that, we won't be able to make the clothing."

"What?"

That sounded like a big problem to me.

It would be near impossible to get her to change into clothes whenever she transformed, and besides, the cost of the clothes would be astronomical.

"Isn't there anything you can do?"

"Well, the material for the jewel can be found in the market . . . but it isn't cheap."

"Ugh . . ."

That was the last thing I wanted to hear.

"Is there any way we could make it?"

"Hm . . . Let me think."

She found a map at the back of the bookshelf and unrolled it on the tabletop.

"I believe, in Melromarc, is only place where the jewels may be found. Here in this cave."

She pointed to the mountainous area in the southwest of the kingdom, and both the guy from the weapon shop and I nodded.

"There is supposed to be a rich vein running through the basement of some ruins here. If you could find it, we'd be able to make the jewel for not much money."

"Sounds like a plan."

It would be dangerous, but we didn't have enough money to think about any other options.

"All right, I'm going with you."

"Are you sure?"

"How else will you know what is good-enough quality?"

I did have a skill that improved my resource appraisal, but it would still be best to have an actual witch choose the jewel.

If we made a good haul, we could sell the remainders for profit. That was obviously a best-case scenario.

"Okay, great. Are you ready to go now?"

"Yes, no problem at all."

"All right then, let's go. And quickly."

We loaded up the carriage with our luggage and had Filo

pull it. Then we all set out for the cave in the southwest of Melromarc.

"Is this the cave?"

I was pointing to what looked like the intimidating entrance to a ruined temple, tucked into the crags of the mountainous region we'd been traversing.

There was a temple built into the ruddy cliffs there . . . and it felt like it must have contained some powerful items within . . . that is, if this were an RPG. I caught myself thinking that way again. I've spent too much time with games!

"No, that's not it. According to local tradition, there was once an evil alchemist who made this temple into his home base."

"You don't say . . ."

"There are rumors that the alchemist was deeply involved in research on a dangerous plant. Apparently that plant is still sealed inside. We will not venture in there. There should be a tunnel bored into the side of the mountain that goes under the temple. That's what we are aiming for."

We all began to scour the area for the tunnel the witch had described.

"Is this it?"

We moved farther down the path to find a giant, fresh crack in the cliff. It was large enough to squeeze inside.

"It could be."

"Mr. Naofumi, should we go in first and check it out?"

I nodded, and we both looked inside.

The interior appeared to be man-made. It was formed from stone but formed into concrete and designed shapes.

What's that? There was an ornate treasure chest sitting at the back of the room. I opened it, but it was empty.

I guess if dungeons were real, this is what they would be like. Of course someone would have been there before you.

"Is it still the alchemist's hideout?"

"Seems to be."

Maybe the alchemist had chosen this spot for his hideout for the very jewels that we had come in search of.

There was a stone pillar, something like a gravestone, right next to the treasure box, and it was inscribed with various symbols. I hadn't studied enough of the language to be able to read it yet.

"Hey, Witch? Can you read this?"

"The letters are very old. 'To he who would break the seal of the seed. It is my desire that this seed never be released into the world. It will play with the people's desire to be freed from famine, granting their wish in the worst way imaginable. The seal is not so easily broken.'"

A seed, huh? So that's what was in this treasure chest. Whatever, it was no concern of mine.

It must have been carried off by some vagrant adventurer at some point—and besides, who had the time to care about this alchemist's half-baked projects?

"I guess this isn't the place."

"I suppose you are correct."

We left the little room and made another pass of the area, and we finally came across the tunnel we were looking for. We went inside.

But . . .

"These monster footprints are very fresh," the witch whispered to herself shortly after entering the tunnel. Her eyes were locked on the ground. I followed her gaze.

These seemed to be the footprints of some type of large carnivore. Come to think of it, I think I had seen similar footprints somewhere.

They reminded me of . . . of the footprints from that giant Chimera that had appeared during the last wave.

"You okay?"

"These make me nervous, I'm not sure if we should continue or not."

"We have to. We don't have a choice."

"If the Shield Hero says so, then it must be the truth. Let's press on."

" . . . "

Filo was sniffing at the tracks.

And then . . .

Ew! She was drooling!

"Let's go, Filo!"

"Okay!"

Filo nodded at Raphtalia's shout, and we set off.

I walked in the front, followed by Raphtalia, the witch, and finally Filo.

It felt like a real adventure. I felt my heart leap, just once, at the excitement of the scene.

"Mr. Naofumi, I have only been using you. Give me money."

I heard Raphtalia's voice echoing off the walls.

"I pretended to become a slave again to gain your trust, but it was all an act. I could stab you right now, from behind. I've wanted to kill you with my own hands."

I turned around to find Raphtalia wincing.

Filo was shouting, "No, Master! Don't leave me!"

What was going on?

"The monsters here are saying things to upset us and get us off our guard. Don't let them fool you."

"What kind of a monster is that?!"

I think I'd seen a monster like that once in a game somewhere. There was a cave with an item in it that was supposed to restore trust to a party whose leader had lost faith in his compatriots. But there was a trap set, a trap to cause vicious infighting.

So that voice just now couldn't have been Raphtalia.

Good. Had that been what Raphtalia had really been thinking, I would have been gutted.

"Master! You need me, right? You need Filo?"

"I guess."

"Yay! I believe you."

"Mr. Naofumi, those words just now were not spoken by me. Let's press onward."

We eventually came upon a monster that looked something like a bat. It was called a Voice Gengar, and it had been making those voices. We fought it, and the witch supported us with magic, so it was an easy win.

Filo ran up a wall and flipped off it, swinging her leg into a powerful kick that brought the bat down. She could really fight. I let the shield absorb the Voice Gengar.

Voice Gengar (bat form) Shield: conditions met
Voice Gengar (bat form) Shield: ability locked: sound wave endurance (small)
Special Effect: Megaphone

Special effect Megaphone? I guess I could tell what that was.

The shield itself wasn't all that great, though I suppose the monster also wasn't that strong, so I shouldn't have expected much.

And yet . . . why did it specify bat form?

It made me wary, and so I strained my ears against the silence of the tunnel. I could hear voices in the distance.

We had no choice but to keep going.

The tunnel had gotten very dark, so I was holding a torch in one hand. Then, suddenly, I couldn't see anything.

"Mr. Naofumi! Prepare yourself!"

Simultaneously, with the shout, I felt a sudden pain.

"Raphtalia?!"

"Mr. Naofumi! Are you all right?!"

"Please die!"

"No! No!"

"Calm down. This is the work of the enemy! They've used magic to darken this passage!"

Damn! That was one killer attack they had. I honestly felt like I'd been stabbed by Raphtalia. And it actually hurt.

Was the attack strong enough to overcome my defense rating?

Had it been Raphtalia . . . she was probably strong enough to hurt me. But the wound felt more like a scratch . . .

"Master! Feed me!"

I heard Filo shouting. Come on now—I was worrying about the scratch I'd gotten, and now Filo was calling out? It was very suspicious. Wasn't there anything we could do?

"Witch, is there anything you can do?"

"I'm starting a spell right now. Just a moment."

I didn't even know if I was speaking to the real witch. What if I believed her, but it was actually the monster talking? This was some cave . . .

That's it! I could use the shield I'd just gotten.

I switched to the Voice Gengar (bat form) Shield and used the special effect Megaphone.

"Hey!"

My voice boomed and echoed down the call, and I heard some strange rustling in response.

"You scared me!"

"Me too," chirped Filo.

"I am the source of all power. Hear me and understand my reasons. Restore our vision."

"Fast Anti-Bind!"

In an instant, the dark hallway became suddenly bright enough to see.

I looked at my feet to see a great number of small, rat-like monsters scurrying around my feet.

Then I looked over at Raphtalia and the others, only to find them beaten up pretty badly.

They must have been attacked in the dark. Of course they'd be beaten up.

I took some healing medicine from my bag and handed it to Raphtalia.

"Witch, do you know any sort of restorative, healing magic?"

"Unfortunately not. I'm not suited for restorative magic."

"Oh . . ."

This wasn't looking good. They had taken some real damage.

Oh hey, that reminds me. I absorbed the monster we'd just defeated, and I unlocked the Voice Gengar (rat form) Shield. Its special effect was the same as the last one, but its equip bonus was Blinding Endurance (small).

Just to be safe, I switched to my Alert Shield. With it equipped, we would be alerted if a monster came within twenty meters of us. I'd wondered how useful a distance like that would be out on the fields, but I now realized that it was a pretty useful distance—if you were indoors or in a dungeon.

We stumbled on through the tunnel for a while before eventually coming upon a vein of ore that glowed dimly in the shadowy hall.

"Kyukiiii!"

A strange voice suddenly filled the air. It was the monster that owned those footprints back at the entrance, and now it was there, guarding the vein of ore.

It was called a Nue. It was so similar to the Chimera.

Nues were like Chimeras in Japanese mythological settings, and they were a type of legendary mythical creature.

It was a monkey's head on a *tanuki's* body, with a tiger's legs and a snake for a tail.

Come to think of it, it looked a lot like the monster Raphtalia and I ran into when we were hunting for the light metal ore and just like the monster we saw during the wave. I'm sure it was just a coincidence, but still—it was creeping me out.

During the wave, it had taken the strength of the other three heroes, plus the support of their parties, to take down that Chimera. Could we take this one here? Just us?

The witch was watching the beast closely. She whispered, "What is a beast from the east doing here?" I guess she meant that the beast was out of its natural habitat.

We could have retreated . . . That wasn't a bad idea at all. I slowly turned my eyes to Raphtalia and the others to signal them to . . . but it was too late.

"I'm going!"

"Okay!"

"Dammit! Don't just rush in!"

But Raphtalia had already run into battle. This was becoming a problem.

I wanted to keep her from getting hurt, but this girl . . .

"I'll support you from behind."

The witch tilted her staff toward the battle and began to chant.

I ran after Raphtalia and Filo.

"Take that!"

"Hiyaaa!"

"Kyukiiii!"

Raphtalia was madly swinging her sword, catching the Nue on its torso. Filo began to kick at the beast's face.

But they weren't getting in anything to approximate a finishing blow. The Nue seemed to be covered in little scratches but was unfazed. It turned its tiger claws toward Raphtalia and Filo.

I wouldn't let it hurt them that easily! I was quicker. And in a flash I was there, covering them with my shield.

"Think for one second before you go rushing in!"

We could have escaped before the beast had even noticed us. But they ruined our chances of escape . . .

"I'm sorry. But now we have to take this thing down!"

"I'm hungry . . ."

"We aren't very strong yet! If you don't think about what fights we can actually win, we're going to end up dead!"

Damn . . . The Nue's claws clipped my shoulder, and I was bleeding.

It really hurt. Now I was pissed.

What?! The Nue's body was suddenly glowing.

"Back off! Hurry!"

"Okay!"

"Master?!"

"I can't back out!"

The Nue's body was now covered in crackling blots of electricity, and it was pressing up against me.

This must have been its special attack.

Could I bear it? I honestly didn't know. But the Nue wasn't going to let me go.

"No!"

Filo kicked the Nue square in the face, and the beast fell back enough for me to jump away.

Filo's kicks were impressively strong.

"Kyukiiiiiii!"

The crackling tongues of electricity all began to gather together on the chest of the Nue.

I was glad that I hadn't been forced to take the brunt of the attack. It seemed like the Nue would be momentarily paralyzed after it lost the attack.

"I am the source of all power. Hear my words and understand them. Burn him!"

"Zweite Fire Place!"

The witch unleashed a blast of fire that covered the Nue.

"Kyukiiiiii!"

Did we win?!

I was hoping it would fall, but the Nue only paused its attack before starting back up again.

"Ugh . . ."

It looked like the thing could run fast if it wanted.

"Master."

"What?!"

"Can I make a big noise too? Like you just did?"

"Sure."

The Voice Gengar Shield had some type of device on the backside of it that would listen to the voice of the user and amplify it.

"Okay, Master! Stop the movement of the monster, like we just did, and then let me make a big noise!"

"What's the point of that?!"

"The monster is very sensitive to sound."

Did she know that because of some kind of mutual monster analysis? I could trust her. In monster hunting games, there were monsters that would show their weak point at a loud sound. It might be a good idea after all, to get in a killing blow . . .

"Witch, you keep up the support magic. Raphtalia, you protect her and watch out for the party."

"But, Mr. Naofumi!"

"I don't have the time to protect both of you! Please, just listen to me!"

"All right."

The Nue was rushing at us. I threw my arms open and stopped its advance.

Dammit! That little monkey-head still had sharp teeth. It was biting me, and it really hurt!

"Kyukiii!"

I took my shield arm, my right arm, and moved it to block the head. My left arm was getting shredded by the tiger claws.

This was driving me crazy. I was covered in scratches. If I were fighting this thing back in Japan, I'd have been mincemeat long ago. Thank goodness for the Legendary Shield. It was going to drop my defense rating, so I didn't want to do it, but I went ahead and changed to the Voice Gengar Shield.

"Go!"

I shouted the sign, and Filo began to inhale a huge amount of air.

"Waaahhhhhhhhhhhhhhhh!"

Crap! My eardrums were about to break!

That's how loud Filo's call was, and that was from this side of the megaphone.

I heard the sound of heavy stumbling in the distance.

"Kyuki?"

Two powerful streams of blood shot from the Nue's ears, and the beast fell over.

Now's our shot!

"Raphtalia! Filo! Witch! Now's our chance! Give it all you've got!"

"Yes!"

"Okay!"

Raphtalia rushed forward and stabbed at the Nue's chest. And Filo . . . Filo started gathering her strength, slowly crouching down to the earth. From under her body, her feet were scratching, scratching, and making a terrifying sound.

"I am the source of all power! Hear my words and understand them! Burn them!"

"Zweite Fire Blast!"

Fireballs flew through the air and collided with the fallen Nue. And that was when it happened.

"Hiyaah!"

Ba-boom! The sound actually exploded and echoed when Filo's charged kick slammed into the Nue. There was so much power in it that the Nue's head exploded into little chunks and the body itself flew back and slammed into the wall.

Ew . . . It was like a gory splatter movie.

"We did it!"

Filo threw both her wings in the air to celebrate our victory, but I personally didn't feel much like celebrating.

I was exhausted and in pain. If Raphtalia and Filo had been a little more careful, we wouldn't have had to fight the thing in the first place, but then . . . there was no point in complaining.

"Well we've won. It seems to have been a child Nue. I think there might have been a rich family somewhere that kept it as a pet, but it escaped and became wild again."

If there were people that would keep something like that as a pet, then this world was worse off than I had imagined.

And did she call this thing a child? I suppose it was a little small . . .

"Feed me!"

Filo stood over the Nue and made to start eating it. Was she just going to start snapping at the dead thing?!

"Stop that!"

"But . . ."

I could unlock new shields with that thing. I couldn't let her just eat it.

I butchered the Nue and absorbed the various parts, unlocking some excellent shields in the process.

But as for status boosts . . . the Chimera had been better.

"Okay, let's rest up for a minute and then get that ore."

There was a vein of glowing ore right there, and it would be easy enough to pry some out with a pickax.

"Good idea. Let's take as much as we can carry."

So we took a break and then set to work prying out ore. Once we had it, we set off.

Oh, of course I also let the shield absorb a little ore too.

But I hadn't filled in the tree enough to unlock anything. And I didn't know what else I needed.

We made our way back to Castle Town, and on the advice

of the witch decided to stop by the apothecary to get some treatment.

Luckily the apothecary knew a place that could treat us, and luckily enough it was cheap to get some restorative magic spells cast on us.

Apparently I could use restorative magic too, so I wanted to hurry up and learn some. That was the rest of our day.

The next day we processed the ore we'd gotten into a proper jewel, which the witch installed on the top of the magical spindle. Just like she'd done the day before, Filo slowly and begrudgingly turned the handle.

"It's boring . . ."

"Just do it. If you finish, then I promise to uphold my end of the bargain."

Honestly, yesterday had been exhausting, and I wanted to relax that day.

"You mean food? Is it gonna be yummy?"

"Yeah."

I kept my word. And I had promised to feed her something delicious, so I would.

"Okay then, I'll do my best!"

She went on turning the squeaky wheel.

"Oh good! She's doing such a good job!"

"Weapon guy. I made a promise to you too. Do you have any time after this?"

"I put up a sign saying I'd be closed until the afternoon, so I have that much time. You gonna get me something good?"

"Something like that. You think you could get me a big sheet of iron?"

"Huh? What do you need something like that for?"

"To cook something."

"Little Hero's gonna cook for us? I don't know if I should look forward to that or not."

"Oh, come on."

He looked disappointed—which annoyed me. Show some gratitude.

"Okay, Raphtalia. Head to the market and get me charcoal, some veggies, and meat. We want enough for five people, but make sure you consider Filo's appetite."

"All right."

I gave her some silver, and she left.

"Yummy food, yummy fooooood!"

Filo was excited now and started turning the spindle wheel faster than before.

That went on for a little while, and then the witch finally asked her to stop.

"That should be enough for now. You can stop."

"If I keep turning it, will I get more yummy food?"

"No. Stop turning it."

"Okaaaaay."

Filo came over to my side in her giant bird form.

"Master . . . yummy food."

"Not yet. We don't have your clothes yet."

"But . . ."

Filo looked very disappointed. But Raphtalia wasn't even back yet, so I couldn't have fed her had I wanted to. I didn't have the things I needed. She was so innocent and free . . . really just like a kid.

"When we leave the magic shop, you need to transform into a human."

"Okay."

Did she really understand? I wasn't sure. Is this what it felt like to have kids? Nah . . .

"I just needed to weave this into cloth, then make the clothes."

The witch held out the thread for me to see.

"I know someone that can take care of turning this into cloth for us."

"He's got an idea, so we're heading out."

"All right then, what should I tell the young lady when she returns from shopping?"

"Just tell her to wait for us at the giant gate where you exit the town."

"Okay."

The weapon shop owner led the way out, and I followed him.

"I'll accept payment later on from the weapon shop!"

"And how much will that be?"

I really wanted to know. That's why I asked.

"For the magic thread? Well the crystals cost quite a lot, but you helped me out and provided me with the materials, so this time let's just call it fair at that."

"Thanks."

She probably knew that I couldn't afford it if she had she asked for 50 pieces silver or something.

So the weapon shop owner and I went to visit a friend of his who said he could turn the thread into cloth for us.

"This is a very rare material indeed. Yes, this might take some thought. But I can probably have it ready for you by this evening. You should take the day and visit a tailor to get measured. I'll bring you the cloth once I have it."

So we went to the tailor.

I couldn't believe how much time and energy we were spending on getting a set of clothes.

"Ooh! What a cute little girl."

The tailor shop was run by a young woman who was wrapped in a scarf and constantly fingered her glasses. She was leaning on the counter.

She seemed kind of plain. I don't know how to describe her. If this were my world, I'd say she looked like the kind of girl who wrote *doujinshi* or something—kind of quiet and geeky.

"She's got little wings too, just like an angel. I've heard there are winged demi-humans too, but they don't look so perfect."

"You think?"

I asked the weapon shop owner what he thought, but he just shrugged.

"Yeah, the winged demi-humans also have other bird-like parts, like their arms and legs. But this girl is just a normal human girl, except for those little wings."

"Huh?"

Filo looked up inquisitively at the tailor.

"Oh yeah, she's actually a monster. She's just transformed into a human right now. When she turns back into a monster, her clothes rip, you see?"

"Ahhh . . .. so you've come to get some magical clothing made, is that right?"

Her glasses flashed. I was sure of it now. Had this been my world, this girl would have been a total *Otaku*.

I knew someone like her back home, who sold her own *doujinshi* at conventions.

She'd lent me some of her participation passes from time to time, and that was how I got to go to some of these conventions and see what they were like. She had been a pretty nice girl.

"She is very pretty, so I think a simple one-piece would work well. If we just add some simple accents that can survive the transformation, that should be enough!"

She unraveled a spiral of measuring tape and set to measuring Filo, who stood there wrapped in my cape.

"I'd love to see her transform!"

"Huh?"

Filo shot me a searching glance. I couldn't think of a way out of it.

"I'm not sure that this room is large enough."

The ceiling only looked to be about two meters high, in which case Filo would slam her head against it in her Filolial form.

"Can I do it while I'm sitting?"

"I guess so."

She sat down and, her eyes on the ceiling, transformed into her original form. The tailor was impressed.

"She's so different! That's even better."

If this girl wasn't shocked by seeing Filo transform, then I felt like she knew what she was doing. We could trust her.

The tailor measured around Filo's neck and started jotting notes about the design.

"Okay, we're all set! I'll just wait for the fabric to show up!"

"This one knows what she's doing."

"Apparently."

She was the kind of person that couldn't stop once the flame was lit. She'd have to focus on the project until it was done.

"I think I can have it done by tomorrow."

"That's fast. But how much will it cost all together? Give me the total please."

"Well, if you are supplying the materials, then . . . probably 40 pieces of silver."

"Filo, are you hearing this? That's 340 pieces of silver I've spent on you now. I'm sure you'll do all you can to help make that money back."

"Okay!"

Did she really get it?

Filo transformed back into a human, and we left the tailor.

We had finished all of our important errands, so we went to the large gate to meet up with Raphtalia.

"Mr. Naofumi, I've bought all the things you requested."

"Filo cost me 340 pieces of silver so far. Raphtalia was way cheaper."

"I wish you wouldn't speak of me as 'cheap.'"

Sigh . . . well, there was nothing left to do but to get down to it.

"Old Dude, go get me that sheet metal. Filo, you go with him and help carry the materials back here."

"Okay!"

"Sure."

Filo set off after the old guy, and they returned quickly, carrying all the luggage.

Why did she transform into a human to lug that luggage around?

Just as I'd hoped, there was a large metal sheet included in the luggage.

"All right! Let's get out of town and head to the riverside."

We walked through the fields until we came to the river-bank.

I set to work arranging stones to hold the sheet of metal. Then I built a fire underneath it.

"Raphtalia, Old Dude, you two watch the fire for me, okay?"

"Um . . . sure."

"Okay."

Whatever he said, the guy made weapons. He should know how to watch a fire.

"What about me?" asked Filo.

"You watch to make sure that we don't get attacked by balloons."

If I'd let Filo help with the fire or cooking, her curiosity would get the better of her, and I'd have a nightmare on my hands. It was much better to give her something else to do.

I started chopping the veggies and meat that Raphtalia had purchased. Then I skewered them on metal prongs.

"Hero Boy, the fire is looking pretty good."

"Great."

Like he said, the metal looked good and hot, so I threw a fatty piece of meat on it to get it good and oiled up. I threw meat and vegetables on the sheet. Then I stuck the skewers around the sheet where they were warmed directly by the flames.

"You're quite the cook!"

I used the knife and a stick I'd found to flip the meat and vegetables to keep them from burning.

"That should be good enough."

That's right: a riverside BBQ. Seemed like a good treat for Filo, if you asked me.

"It's ready, Filo."

"Yay!"

Filo was already drooling from the smell, but she waited until I handed her a fork before she lunged at the meat.

"Yummy! It's so yummy!"

She kept going, eating more and more.

"Hey now, this is for everyone. Don't eat it all yourself!"

"Fine . . ."

Her cheeks were stuffed with food when she nodded. Did she really understand?

"Just like that. Raphtalia, Old Guy, dig in!"

"All right."

"Thanks."

They held out their plates, and I piled meat and veggies up for them.

"Whoa, this is damn good! Who knew that just cooking meat would make it so good."

"Yes, Mr. Naofumi's food is often strange but delicious."

"I'll take that as a compliment."

The old guy turned his head in thought.

"I wonder if it's because of my cooking skill?"

"You mean from the Shield?"

"That's what I was thinking."

"What a mysterious and powerful Shield. I'm jealous."

"I can't take it off. It's actually pretty inconvenient."

And I couldn't attack at all . . .

"You must be a lot stronger than you used to be."

"I wonder."

We were supposed to travel the world, let the Legendary Weapons absorb different monsters and materials, and get stronger.

To be honest, I still had no idea how much there was out there to see.

I didn't know how much the shield had to grow to be complete.

But even if I ignored it and just lounged around, the next wave was still coming. I didn't even know how many times the waves were going to come.

There had already been two. Would they end after the fifth, the tenth . . . the hundredth?

Whatever the answer, I had to do what I could.

That reminds me. I've been wondering about this Curse Series Shield.

When they were about to take Raphtalia from me, the shield was absorbed by something and the Curse Series Shield was unlocked. I looked for it on my skill tree but hadn't been able to find it.

I opened the help screen.

Curse Series: should not be touched

That's all there was written at first. But after I looked around a few times, the words vibrated as if shocked, and they changed.

Curse Series: delivers extraordinary power and grief to its holder: should not be touched

I was still unable to find the shield, so I decided to ignore it for the time being.

It must have been the type of weapon that only appeared as an option when you really needed it. It was some kind of conditional shield.

"Master! We ran out of meat."

"What?!"

Sure enough, there was no more meat. The skewers had all been picked clean too.

Now there were only veggies left.

"Is that it? But I'm still hungry," cried Filo.

I sighed.

"Then run into the woods and catch five Usapils. I'll cook them for you."

"Okay!"

Filo ran, full speed, into the woods.

"That was damn good. Mighty fine meal."

"If you think so, subtract the cost of that cloth from the bill."

"If I did that, I'd be in the hole, Hero Boy."

So we spent the rest of the day there, cooking veggies and meats by the riverside. The sun started to set.

And Filo had managed to catch ten Usapils.

I actually wasn't able to eat very much at all. I spent all my time butchering Usapils and cooking for everyone else.

Chapter Ten: Traveling Merchant

The next morning we went to the tailor, and that *Otaku* girl was waiting for us at the door, a wide smile on her face.

"It took me all night, but I finished! I think you're going to like it."

She'd stayed up all night, but she was still chipper—practically bouncing off the walls. She ran back behind the counter and returned with Filo's new clothes in hand.

It was basically a white one-piece dress, but there was a large blue ribbon in the center. It was fringed here and there with blue ribbon for contrast. You could tell with one glance that it was well-made and made full advantage of the materials.

It had a "simple is best" esthetic, the sort of clothing that chooses its wearer.

"Master! Am I supposed to wear this?"

"Yeah."

"Yay!"

She threw off the cape and stood there completely naked.

"Stop that."

"But . . ."

Raphtalia stopped her and led her into the back of the shop.

"Okay, so try transforming into your monster form."

I could hear the tailor's voice echoing in the back room.

"Why?"

"If you don't, the ribbon will dig into you."

"Oh no!"

That was an odd threat to make.

"Okay!"

I heard a loud thump as she transformed, and then . . .

"Yup . . . I knew it would look good."

She sounded rather self-satisfied.

"Okay, let's get going!"

"Yay!"

All the girls came out from the back room together, and I got my first look at Filo.

She was already a cute girl. But with the clothes and her white wings, she really did look like an angel. She was in a white one-piece dress with a large blue ribbon on her chest as an accent. She was like a little 2D child angel heroine!

"Master!"

"Huh?"

"How do I look?"

"It suits you well."

This *Otaku* girl really knew what she was doing. Who else could have come up with a design that worked so well with Filo's appearance and specs.

"Ehehe."

Filo looked a little embarrassed, but she played with the fringe on the skirt and spun in a little circle.

We left the tailor shop and decided to head back to Riyute. To do so, we had to get Filo to pull our carriage. When Filo transformed into a Filolial, the clothes would disappear, but the ribbon would remain as a collar around her neck.

The clothes were expensive, but there had clearly been a lot of thought put into them.

"Oh, Shield Hero!"

We were leaving Castle Town when we happened to come across the witch from the magic shop.

"Are you on your way to Riyute?"

"Yeah."

"I'm on my way there also. Could I trouble you for a ride?"

She was smiling.

We were going there anyway, and she had gone out of her way to help us, so it didn't seem right to turn her down.

"I can't guarantee a smooth ride, but you're welcome to come with us."

"I did ride in it two days ago."

"Oh yeah, that's right."

Raphtalia had learned to fight her motion sickness by watching the horizon.

"Thank you, Hero."

The witch climbed up into the carriage.

"All right, Filo! Let's go, but take it slow."

"Okay!"

All the pedestrians stopped to stare at Filo as we passed. They probably weren't used to seeing talking monsters. We proceeded down the street slowly to the tapping of Filo's feet.

It felt like the last few days had been so busy. I mean, it always felt like the days were busy, but these last days had felt even more so. And to think it was all Filo's fault.

As for the witch . . . Well, I wanted to learn magic, but if I had asked right then, I couldn't be sure how she would respond.

And I felt guilty for not studying as much as I should have.

The witch had given us those books, so I wanted to repay her kindness by studying from them. Yes, I'd have to devote more time to it.

I didn't know all the ins and outs of this world like the other heroes did. So I had to be learning new things all the time. Even still, I needed to give special priority to learning the writing system and to understanding the recipes I'd gotten. If I didn't, it would be a waste.

"Huh . . . it's so light."

Filo was yawning as she walked, and now she started to mutter to herself.

There were three people in the carriage, and she was complaining that it was too light?

This was good. I already had an idea what I wanted to try . . . and I'd need Filo to do it.

When we arrived at Riyute, the witch gave me 25 pieces of silver.

"What's this for?"

"For the ride."

"Oh . . . Thanks."

Maybe we could make money off this too?

Riyute was still invested in rebuilding. I checked in at the inn, and the innkeeper gave us a friendly greeting.

"Okay, let's get started on Raphtalia's motion sickness training, also known as lumber transport duty."

We'd agreed to help carry lumber in exchange for meat.

"Huh?!"

Raphtalia looked upset. Then again, she was going to have to fight motion sickness all day.

"We're going to be carried around by Filo from now on, so you better get used to it."

"Pfft. Fine."

"Okay!"

"Filo, you're going to do the pulling."

"Okay!"

Apparently Filolials really did enjoy pulling carriages. She was so excited her eyes were shining.

"Um . . . did you have some kind of plan?"

"Yes, I was thinking of becoming a traveling merchant. The local governor suggested it to me."

"A traveling merchant?"

"Yeah. We don't have all that many products, but I would focus on medicine and transport. We could cover a good range."

"Hm . . ."

Raphtalia didn't seem very interested. To be fair, it wasn't like I had confidence that we would succeed. But we were about to start traveling anyway, so it seemed like a natural idea.

"Which means, if we started transporting things, that Filo will need to run at pretty much full speed. I can't have you getting sick on me all the time."

"I understand that, but . . ."

"Oh, c'mon. I know a good, smooth place that should be pretty easy to start with. You can get used to it there."

"You know a place like that?"

"Sure."

And so, at the start of the day's work, I put Raphtalia somewhere she wouldn't get sick . . . on Filo's back.

"Master, you can ride there anytime you want . . . but why do I have to give her a ride?"

Filo grumbled to herself as Raphtalia climbed up on her back.

"I feel the same way. This is so embarrassing."

When Filo was in her Filolial Queen form, she was like a

giant owl, which made sitting on her back look a little ridiculous.

"You comfy?"

"Yup, feels good!"

Maybe because this was her "real form," Filo seemed perfectly content.

"Okay then, let's go!"

"Yay! I'll help you so much! I'll be just as useful as Raphtalia!"

"It's not a competition!"

"But I won't lose!"

Filo, with Raphtalia on her back, started to pull the carriage.

With the weight of the carriage and us passengers, it must have been pretty heavy, but not heavy enough for Filo, apparently. What did they have to fight about? I spent the time on the road with my book open, studying the writing system and trying to translate the intermediate recipe book.

. . . Tap, tap.

. . . . . . Tap, tap.

The rhythmic sound of Filo's footsteps was excellent music for absorbing myself in the erudite and obtuse world of foreign character sets and language. But then I heard them . . .

"Why? Why in that form?"

"Huh? Because I want my master to be pleased!"

. . . . Tap, tap.

"He'll just be mad. You better stop."

"But, Master . . . Master likes people like you, doesn't he?"

Huh? I looked up to see Filo transformed back into a human, with Raphtalia still on her back. Raphtalia looked very uncomfortable, and she was talking to Filo, trying to get her to change back.

Some adventurers passed us on the street, and they pointed in our direction and started whispering among themselves.

"Stop acting like that! People are going to start gossiping!"

I could hear the rumors now. I bought a slave and put her on the back of another little girl and forced them to pull my luggage carriage down the street. That wouldn't reflect well on me at all.

"Really? What's wrong?"

"Don't pull the carriage as a human."

"Fiiine."

She gave a disappointed nod and turned back into a monster. It must have been boring for her or something.

Raphtalia wasn't sick yet, so that was good. It was time to pick up the pace a little.

"Okay, Filo! Let's speed up."

"Yay!"

Raphtalia let out a yelp, then hunkered down and grabbed tight to Filo's feathers.

That should get us where we were going faster.

We spent the next few hours working on Raphtalia's motion sickness prevention practice.

Chapter Eleven: Travel by Carriage

A few days passed, and the local governor gave us a new carriage as a present. The whole village gathered to be there when we received it, and there was a party at which everyone cheered for us.

If you wanted to move a Filolial, you needed a carriage . . . or something like that.

"Thank you."

"You've done so much to help us. We're just sorry that we can't do more for you."

The villagers were all smiling as they helped me load up the carriage.

I couldn't let them spoil me, even if they wanted to. Still, I needed to honestly express my gratitude.

"Thank you for saying that."

"You'll be trying your hand at being a traveling merchant?"

"Yeah."

I didn't know whether or not I would be successful with it or not. But I was lucky enough to have Filo with us, so it seemed stupid not to put her to work.

"Huh? A carriage!"

Filo had been running around and playing as a human and was surprised to see the new carriage.

"Am I going to pull this?"

Her eyes were flashing with joy.

"That's right. You're going to pull this thing, and we're going to travel all over the country."

"Really?!"

She squealed in excitement.

Didn't she realize she'd have to lug a heavy carriage around? I don't see what was so exciting about that . . .

"So we are really going to do it?" Raphtalia muttered, sounding depressed at the prospect.

She hadn't quite gotten control over her queasy stomach, so the idea of traveling by carriage was not terribly appealing.

"It might be tough at first, but you'll get used to it."

"Okay."

I looked over at Filo and looked her over carefully.

"Filo, what's your job?"

"Let's see . . . I'm supposed to pull the carriage and go where you tell me to go, Master."

"Right."

"And if we meet that Spear guy, I'm supposed to kick him."

"Exactly."

"That last part's not true!"

Raphtalia had her arms crossed like she was going to right all the wrongs in the world.

"What? Why are you looking at me like I'm weird?"

If we see Motoyasu, Filo would kick him. What was weird about that?

Oh well, I couldn't entertain every one of her complaints.

"All right! This is the official start of our traveling merchant life. I'll hide in the carriage. Raphtalia, when we get to a new town, you start selling our wares from the front."

"Oh, all right . . ."

My poor reputation was still alive and well out in the world beyond Riyute. If I were in charge of the sales, we'd never sell anything—who would want to negotiate with a criminal? It only made sense to put Raphtalia in charge.

Raphtalia was pretty, and she had the personality for it. She wouldn't be shy.

"Shall we be on our way?"

"Oh, Hero."

"Huh? What is it?"

"Please, take this . . ."

The governor handed me a piece of parchment.

"What's this?"

"The commercial bill of passage that we discussed earlier."

"Oh yeah . . ."

With the bill of passage in hand, I'd be able to sell my things in different towns without having to pay the local governors any tariffs. It would make my life much easier. Now, whether or not these local governors should really be charging the heroes to pass through their towns . . . that's another story altogether.

I mean, Motoyasu clearly thought that way.

"Travel safely."

"Thanks. We'll be on our way now."

"I hope we can help you out more in the future. You've done so much for us."

"Just don't push yourselves too hard."

"Okay!"

And so we left Riyute behind and started our new lives as traveling merchants.

The first thing we tried was selling various medicines.

We didn't have a huge selection prepared, so we set our prices lower than the typical market price.

We started with healing medicine and nutritional drinks. They were both better than just your average medicines and drinks, and so I set the price a little higher than our other products.

Then we would stock up on herbs and supplies and leave for the next village—I'd use our time on the road to compound new medicines.

Filo was really fast, so we almost made it to the next town in a single day, though there were times that we had to stay camped in the wilderness. On nights like that, we would stop the carriage, build a fire, and have dinner under the stars.

"Master! There's room next to me! Come sleep with me!"

We'd finished eating, and Filo transformed back into her monster form and was tapping the spot on the ground next to her.

"It's too hot sleeping next to you . . ."

Filo still wanted to sleep with me every night. I'd ordered her not to turn into a monster when we were at an inn, so she took the opportunity whenever we camped out.

Granted, we were alone out there, so there was no one she could inconvenience . . .

"Filo, you sure do like Mr. Naofumi, don't you?"

"Yeah! I like him even more than you do, Big Sister!"

"Don't call me that!"

Her problem was with "big sister"?

"Then what should I call you?"

"Hm . . . how about 'Mommy'? I was there when you hatched from your egg, and I've known you the whole time! Seems fitting, doesn't it?"

"I dunno . . . Big Sister!"

They kept fighting among themselves like they couldn't decide whether they were friends or enemies.

Filo was just like a little kid, so she couldn't help but get too serious about things.

Actually, I guess she really was a little kid. And she acted like one.

"Okay, okay, both of you should get to bed. When my shift is up, I'm going to wake you!"

"Stop treating me like a little kid!"

"Yes! Mr. Naofumi, you treat me like a child!"

"Oh, whoops! I keep forgetting how grown up the both of you are!"

"You don't mean it!"

"Yeah, Master! You liar!"

But they really were like children. And I'd decided to be a parent to them both.

"I want to help you keep watch, Master!"

Filo picked up some rocks and started rubbing them together over random grasses in a loose approximation of my mortar and pestle.

"Ew! It smells funny!"

"Yeah, it does."

If you could make medicine from random grasses, it wouldn't be so hard, would it?

"Why isn't it working?"

"You can learn some things just by watching, but others take a little more practice."

"Is that why you can't pull a carriage?" she asked.

"Why do I have to pull a carriage?" I said.

"Why are you and I different?" she kept on.

"What's wrong with being different?" I replied.

Just like a kid . . . she'd attack anything she could think of.

If we just kept going back and forth with questions, then eventually she'd get confused and have to give up.

"Argh . . . Master is so . . . so stupid!"

"Who are you calling stupid?!"

We kept at it for a while, and I was able to get some work done too.

Chapter Twelve: Rumors of the Heroes

"Huh?"

We were on our way to the next village and had been traveling for about an hour, which I'd spent working in the back, when I noticed a strange sound.

Coming from the other side of the carriage wall came the sound of a man desperately out of breath. I poked my head out to see a flustered man running beside us, a bag in his outstretched hand.

"What are you in such a rush for?"

I figured that showing curiosity in times like this could easily lead to a sale.

We slowed the carriage down so that I could hear what the man had to say.

"I have to get to the village across the mountains . . ."

"You're running to the village over the mountains?"

Apparently his parents were sick and he was running to get medicine for them. Filo had just overtaken him on the road.

"Yes, and without a minute to spare!"

"Filo, if you ran as fast as you could, how long would it take to get there?"

"Lemme think . . . Well, I could go faster if I didn't have to pull the carriage . . ."

"Fine."

I looked over to Raphtalia, and she nodded immediately, already understanding what I meant to say.

"We'll take you there for a silver piece."

"What?"

The man was shocked.

"But I was just going to buy medicine . . . See, I don't have enough money . . ."

"You can just give us something worth a silver piece or just bring us medicinal herbs the next time you see us. Of course, if you don't keep your promise . . ."

"Oh, well, if that's okay then . . ."

"Great! That settles it! Filo?"

"Okay!"

I moved over onto Filo's back and pulled the man up to sit with me.

"Whoa!"

The man was surprised, but Filo covered him with her wings and took off at full speed.

Raphtalia was waving to us from the carriage.

"Here we go!"

"Oh!"

Filo might have been shaped like an owl now, but it had done nothing to slow her speed.

Before we knew it, we had already arrived at the man's house.

"That was so fast!"

"You better hurry up and get them their medicine. Careful now!"

"Okay!"

The man went into the house, and I followed him inside. We hadn't finished discussing my payment.

It was an average farmer's house. I could hear violent coughing coming from somewhere inside.

"Ma . . . It's medicine. You gotta drink it."

I followed the sound of the voices and came across the young man giving medicine to two older people, both with pale faces.

I didn't know what kind of medicine it was, but it seemed to be more effective than the medicines I was accustomed to.

"Hey. I'll take care of administering the medicine. Why don't you go boil some water and make them something good?"

"Are you sure?"

"Yeah, I'm just waiting to see what happens."

I took the medicine from the man and, supporting the weight of the old woman, gently gave her some medicine.

I hoped that the medicine efficacy skill booster I'd learned before would work.

Cough . . . Cough . . .

The old woman took the medicine and managed to swallow some of it.

The woman was suddenly enveloped in a shower of glowing light. Apparently that signified that the medicine had been effective. She even looked healthier. Some color had returned to her pale face, and she seemed to be coughing less than she had been.

"Just try and relax. Your family will be back with food soon."

She managed a weak smile and then lay back down.

"Now then . . ."

I left the room and went into the kitchen.

"Did they take the medicine?"

"Yes, and it seems to have worked."

He sighed deeply, as though a great weight had been removed from his shoulders.

"I'll be back later, so make sure you have my money."

"Okay."

I left the house, found Filo, and quickly road back to where we had left the carriage.

When we arrived back at the village, the man was there waiting for us, looking tense.

"Um . . ."

"What is it?"

We talked as we unloaded the luggage from the carriage.

"My mother seems to be doing much better . . . but just who are you?"

"You don't need to know."

If he knew my name, he'd instantly associate me with the bad rumors that have been going around. And he would start to doubt me.

"Please just tell me your name."

"I'm not obligated to. The medicine worked, right? So bring me a piece of silver or something worth that much."

"All right!"

He ran back to the house, flipped through some materials, and then came back out with some food.

"So that's it, huh? Fine. Well, keep an eye out for us, okay?"

"Yes! Thank you very much!"

The man looked very happy.

I suppose it's a bit of a digression, but sometime later on we actually did come back to this village. The old lady was very energetic, almost too much so.

I went back to my studies in the back of the carriage. I was trying to read the intermediate medicine recipe book. The recipe book seemed easier to understand than the magic book, so I was starting with that one. But after I dedicated a bunch of time to translating a recipe, I found out that it was a medicine I already knew . . . I was disappointed.

Come to think of it, I had been pretty neglectful of my studies up until now. I'd been so busy for the last month that I hadn't had time to think about it, but if I ever made it out of here alive, I'd have to say something to my brother, who had worn himself out studying too hard.

"Mr. Naofumi, I think we are pretty much done here for today."

We'd arrived just past noon, and now evening was approaching.

"Are there any parcels or letters that we could take to the next village?"

"I've already collected them."

I climbed out of the carriage and helped load up the luggage.

Granted, there were only certain kinds of people that would give their luggage to a traveling merchant they'd never met. It was mostly cheap things that people wouldn't be too upset to lose. Even still, we were able to make some good change.

We traveled this way for a while, moving from village to village and town to town.

Whenever someone wanted restorative medicine, I would give it to them myself, and that way they could take advantage of my medicine efficacy skill.

After we'd been at it for two weeks or so, we began to get a bit of a reputation as the merchants with the weird bird that sold everything.

When we had made a good name for ourselves, people became much more trusting, and more and more pedestrians came to ask us for rides. So before long our profits started to rise.

There were some really good things about the traveling merchant's lifestyle.

The first was that I could sell the medicine that I made while we were on the road. The second was that I was able to absorb any monsters that we came across on our travels. Of course, all I really ever got out of it was typical status boosts.

One other thing I learned after we started traveling was that monsters were very different depending on the locale. Considering that I could grow stronger by absorbing a variety of different monsters, starting this traveling gig was turning out to be a really good arrangement.

The other good thing was that I was now in a position to hear all sorts of gossip.

I'd had no idea for the longest time, but now I was able to make a good guess where the other heroes, Motoyasu, Ren, and Itsuki, had based themselves.

Motoyasu seemed to be out to the southwest of the castle, where he had apparently saved a starving village by breaking the seal on some kind of legendary crop. He must have known to go there since he knew everything about the place already. It actually reminded me a lot of the place we'd been to, where we fought the Nue.

Ren had gone to the southeast of the castle, but apparently

he would go anywhere that was inhabited by tough monsters. I'd heard various tales of his exploits—like that he'd defeated a violent dragon somewhere out to the east.

As for Itsuki . . . I wasn't sure what he wanted to do, but he had gone with some adventurers that had visited the kingdom seeking help. He went with them to a country in the north, where the government was corrupt. He fought with the resistance to overthrow an evil lord.

Having said that, Itsuki's story was missing the most details, so I couldn't really be sure of anything. I'd only heard vague references to him as "that adventurer with the strong bow" and so on.

All of this sounded a lot like something I'd read before coming to this world, something I'd read in *The Records of the Four Holy Weapons*.

Anyway, so that's what our travels were like.

At the end of the two weeks, our stats were looking like this:

Naofumi: LV 34
Raphtalia: LV 37
Filo: LV 32

I guess it was because she was a monster, but Filo was certainly leveling up quickly.

Filo was now much stronger, physically, than she had been. While she used to use both hands (wings?) to pull the carriage, she now only used one and yawned the whole time.

Naturally, I tried to get her to try harder, but she only protested.

"But it's so light that I lose my motivation!"

Whatever.

Afterward, all the shields that I got while traveling only unlocked status boosters.

If there were any interesting shields . . . well, there was this one:

Crystal Ore Shield: ability unlocked: equip bonus: fine crafting 1

We'd come into a booming mining town, and there was a poor-quality crystal lying there. I let the shield absorb it, and that was what I got.

It seemed like a skill that could lead to some serious money-making possibilities, but I didn't have enough information to go trying it out just yet.

I tried polishing the crystal ore, but it just broke and crumbled, so it must need to be combined with something else in a recipe. Either that or I was just doing it wrong.

Regardless, I still needed to translate that book the apothecary had given me.

Sure, if I'd spent two weeks on it, it should have been simple enough to read. And I'd had the thing for close to three weeks now, so I should have been able to glean some information from it.

Antidote, weed killer, healing salve, restorative medicine (I'd already made that), nutritional drink (I'd made that too), gunpowder, acidic water, magical water, soul healing medicine, and insecticide were the recipes I'd been able to figure out, and after I went through them all, the book was over. Apparently you could alter the effectiveness of these basic intermediate medicines by mixing them with different additives. It was all rather vague, so I wouldn't say that I really had a handle on it. Even still—I was starting to realize that the recipes the apothecary had given me were pretty average for intermediate level.

Well, I'd been able to figure out the book, so I didn't think I'd need it anymore. I let the shield absorb it. This was the shield I unlocked:

Book Shield: ability unlocked: equip bonus: magic power up (small)

I thought for sure the shield would unlock some intermediate medicine recipes, but I was wrong.

And on top of that, the shield's defense rating was really low!

It happened the day after I finished translating the recipe book.

We came upon a monster called Torrent, defeated it, and I absorbed it into my shield.

Torrent Shield: conditions met
Blue Torrent Shield: conditions met
Black Torrent Shield: conditions met

Torrent Shield: ability locked: equip bonus: plant classification 2
Blue Torrent Shield: ability locked: equip bonus: intermediate compounding recipe 2
Black Torrent Shield: ability locked: equip bonus: rookie compounding

Intermediate recipes? Was this some kind of joke? I just finished translating that book!

Well, at least I'd only done up until the healing salve. The last time a shield unlocked recipes, it was from a Mush, so I guess plant-based monsters would yield recipes. Even still, after I'd put in all that work—here they were: unlocked just like that.

The antidote, weed killer, and healing salve could be made

from grasses, but I didn't even know where to get the materials to make anything like gunpowder.

The apothecary's notes made it seem like you could make substitutions in the case of gunpowder. There was something called Snappy Grass that could substitute, so I did that and tried to make some gunpowder.

It was like a crumbly powder, something like ash that could burn. I gathered it into a bag and made a makeshift bomb.

I set flame to it and planned to throw it at an enemy. It started crackling, but then I dropped it at my feet!

I was scared, but fortunately it didn't produce anything you could really call an "explosion."

The acidic water needed to be stored in a glass bottle. It was a liquid that apparently was only slightly less acidic than sulfuric acid. It wasn't made from grasses but was made by taking different natural ores and adding them to water . . . or something like that. I hadn't made it yet, so I can't say for sure . . . but what kind of person would want such a thing and what would they want it for? Anyway, I could make some just to absorb into the shield.

The Magic Power Water would restore your consumed magic points when you drank it. But the materials necessary to make it were pretty hard to get your hands on.

If you made it with commercially available grasses, it would cost a small fortune. If we were going to go through the effort of making it, it would be better to sell it than to use it. Just like the Magic Power Water, the Soul Healing Medicine would also replenish the user's SP. But Raphtalia and Filo didn't seem to understand what SP was, and they said it just tasted delicious, but like normal water.

The insecticide was easy. You just mixed various herbs that insects hated and either clumped them into a solid or dissolved them in water for a liquid.

So out of my new recipes, the ones that would be good for production and sales were the antidote, the healing salve, and the insecticide.

And the weed killer would be good too. You could make so much of it from so little material that all I'd need to do was give some thought as to where to sell it. I could let the shield absorb the leftovers.

Anti-Poison Shield: conditions met
Gurihosato Shield: conditions met
Medicine Shield: conditions met
Plant Fire Shield: conditions met
Killer Insect Shield Alpha: conditions met

Anti-Poison Shield: ability locked: equip bonus: defense power 5
Gurihosato Shield: ability locked: equip bonus: attack from plant enemies reduced by 5%

Medicine Shield: ability locked: equip bonus: medicine effective range expansion (small)

Plant Fire Shield: ability locked: equip bonus: fire resistance (small)

Killer Insect Shield Alpha: ability locked: equip bonus: attack from insect enemies reduced by 3%

I bet the original ability for the Anti-Poison Shield was Poison Resistance (medium). But I'd already learned that skill from the Chimera Viper Shield, so it must have changed to accommodate that.

The Medicine Shield would increase some kind of range, though I wasn't sure exactly what it meant.

It could have meant that the range for any particular medicine would be increased, but it could also mean the *number* of people it could work on would increase.

What was Gurihosato? It seemed like the name of some kind of weed killer product. As for Killer Insect Shield Alpha, I imagined that you could produce a beta version or something by changing up the kinds of grasses that you used in the concoction.

The effect of cutting 3% from the damage of certain kinds of enemies seemed pretty useful to me.

The real problem was trying to read the magic book. It was very difficult.

Lately it seemed that Raphtalia was starting to get the hang of it. She'd produced certain effects that looked like they were on the right path. She'd been able to produce an orb of light that would float before her for a few seconds. Considering I was the Shield Hero, I didn't look so great in comparison.

Filo could use her transformation magic too, so I asked Filo about it after Raphtalia had gone to bed.

It was kind of hard to think of what she did as magic, per se, but I thought it would be good to hear what she thought anyway.

"Yeah, so I, um . . . I just think about my power, like way down inside, right? And I just, like, think about what I want to be and, uh . . . then I be it!"

Right. Whatever. At least I figured out that she wasn't doing it as the result of some reasoned process.

But what if I could read the book but still found myself unable to practice the magic? I'd heard that magic can be funny like that.

And I came from a world that didn't have any magic at all, so if it turned out that I wasn't able to use it that would be . . . upsetting. I had to learn it. I just had to.

Not to please the witch from the magic shop . . . but to stay alive.

When the waves came, there wasn't much need for me to participate in the fighting. Besides, who knew how I would be treated after the enemy had been vanquished? The best job for me would be to protect the nearby villages and towns. And when I was doing that, being able to use magic or not, that might decide whether or not I made it through the day alive.

I could have bought a crystal ball . . . but if I could learn magic from this book for free, then that seemed like a better way to go. So lately, when we were on the road, I had the magic book in one hand, and I tried to read it.

I asked Raphtalia how she did it, and she said that she synchronized her magic power with the words on the page, and her soul reacted . . . Just like Filo's had been, her explanation was impossible to follow.

Granted, I could follow it better than Filo's . . . but what was "magic power" anyway? Did it mean they could feel it, like a sixth sense?

My head was filled with questions like that, and it was driving me crazy.

Well anyway, that's how we spent those last two weeks.

Chapter Thirteen: Take Everything but Life

"Oh wow . . . To think that I'm riding in a carriage pulled by a bird-god! What a treat!"

"Bird-god?"

A passing merchant had asked for a ride to the next town down the road, so we had given him a ride.

"Haven't you heard of it? Hm, well . . . Hey, aren't you the owner of this carriage? Even if you hide, I can tell."

He had been chatting with Raphtalia, but now he pointed his finger at me.

We'd been pretending that Raphtalia was in charge, and I stayed in the back making medicines.

"That's true . . ."

"You are famous around town. They say there's a cart pulled by a bird-god that showers people with miracles everywhere it goes."

The carriage was rattling down the road. I turned to look at Filo.

So people thought she was a god! In truth she was a hungry little pig, spoiled everywhere she went.

But what was this miracle the guy was talking about?

Hm?

"Gwehhhhh!"

Filo looked suddenly startled, and she took off running.

"Whoa!"

The merchant, Raphtalia, and I all flew out of our seats and had to throw our arms out to stabilize ourselves.

"Ahhhh!"

"Yasuuuuuu!"

RATTLE, RATTLE!

The carriage was rattling so loudly that we couldn't hear what was happening outside. Sometimes Filo would just run off like that for no real reason. This was probably the fourth time since we'd started this traveling gig. She kind of just did whatever she wanted.

"I'm not the only passenger here. Take it easy, Filo!"

"Okay! But that's not it . . . Gweh!"

We whispered to each other so as not to be overheard by the merchant. We didn't want to attract more attention than necessary, as that would only spell trouble. But I felt like people were paying attention to us anyway.

The merchant was already staring at me with a shocked expression on his face.

"I'd heard she could understand language. That's amazing!"

"I think so too."

Think about it: if people were so surprised that she could understand language, what would they think about her being able to speak? Her specs must have been really high.

I should think about it as a potential that monsters have . . . when you look at it that way, she must have been very rare indeed.

"Even still, we're just normal traveling merchants. We give people rides now and then, but nothing out of the ordinary."

"People are saying that a holy man arrives in a carriage and blesses the sick with special medicine. They are saying you cure people."

"Really?"

Sure, it was pretty good medicine, but if you saved up a little, anyone could have bought it. But I'd discovered that you could tweak the recipe specifically for the needs of the patient as well. The original recipe worked on everything, but not particularly well. I'd been adding different herbs to the recipe to help it treat more ailments.

I'd made it to work on fevers, lung infections, and skin infections. Still, it was just one medicine.

The method had been written out explicitly in the intermediate recipe book. The recipes I'd gotten from the shield had also suggested a few recipe tweaks.

"It's just normal medicine though."

I opened a box and took out the medicine to show him.

"This is the miracle medicine?"

He lifted the lid from the jar and sniffed at it.

"Well, it does smell like normal medicine. That's for sure."

"You can tell?"

Was he an apothecary? I was curious, so I asked him. But he shook his head.

"No, I can just kind of tell."

Sure he could.

"So what sort of merchant are you?"

"I'm a jeweler."

Right, a jeweler . . . I guess they existed in this world too.

I guess that he normally sold necklaces and stuff to rich people.

"Jewels, eh? So I guess you tend to work with wealthy people."

If he was carrying around expensive jewels and looking for customers, he would probably need some powerful protection. So it was odd that he was traveling alone.

"You hit where it hurts."

He gave a light chuckle and then went on.

"Oh, I sell everything there is, from small to large. You could call me an accessories dealer."

"What's the difference?"

"Care to take a look at my products?"

He took out a large bag of accessories for my inspection.

I looked inside. It was filled with broaches and necklaces. And bracelets.

But it looked like most of them were made from iron or bronze. And there were jewels embedded . . . technically. They weren't so nice. The word "jewel" seemed too grandiose to describe them.

"I mostly just sell cheap stuff."

"Huh . . . Did you run into some kind of trouble?"

"Not exactly . . . my current product line was from a rather poor adventurer."

"Huh."

According to the accessories dealer, different accessories could be imbued with magic to give different effects to their wearer.

"And how much does one of those things sell for?"

"Right . . . right . . . Well, this iron bracelet will raise the wearer's attack power, and it goes for about 30 pieces of silver."

That was pretty expensive. I couldn't sell any of my medicines for near that much.

"If we were to apply magic to it we could sell it for near 100 pieces of silver."

"Really?"

"Of course."

Heh. That might be worth thinking about.

I had pretty much reached the ceiling of what I could accomplish by selling medicines. We were close to selling out, and that was making us some money, but not a lot. I was also thinking about selling some to different apothecaries—and that wasn't good for much profit. If I started collecting materials to make more, I would run out of time.

I could have started before I'd moved on to selling things, but if you make things and collect things at the same time, your efficiency starts to go down.

"You a craftsman?"

"I suppose . . . It's easy enough to just make the pieces . . . but once I go ahead and add the magic power to them, yeah, I guess I'm a craftsman of sorts."

That made sense. He'd make the pieces, and once they had magic put into them they would give their wearer certain powers.

But how do you imbue something with magic? That was the trick . . .

I didn't like the sound of it. "Imbue with magic." That had been all over my medicine recipes, and I'd seen it pop up in the recipe for magic water too.

It meant that if you couldn't use magic, you couldn't make any of those medicines or objects.

"Master! Something is coming!"

Filo sounded tense, and after calling out to me, she stopped in place.

Raphtalia and I quickly jumped from the carriage to see what was going on.

We saw someone walking out of the deep forest.

There was a crowd, and they all had weapons in hand. They didn't look friendly, and they were coming straight for us.

They were all dressed differently, but they all had armor on. They were bandits, probably coming down from the mountains.

"Bandits!"

The accessory dealer let out a shrill shout.

"Ehehehe . . . leave the valuables behind and just be on your way."

Hah . . . what a cliché.

I'd heard of this kind of thing before . . . Why didn't they just sneak up and attack?

But Filo had seen them first, so they must have just decided to give up on the surprise and come right at us. They must have thought they could win. They looked haughty. Either that or they had another plan.

That reminds me. When we were in the last village, I'd heard about some cruel faction of bandits forming out in the wilderness.

"We know all about you! And we know that you've got a jeweler in there too."

The bandits were gathered in a crowd, and they were all shouting at us. I looked at the accessory merchant in the back of the carriage.

"Didn't you say that you weren't carrying anything of much value?"

"Yes . . . nothing like that at the moment."

He slowly slipped his hand into his pocket and seemed to be fingering something there.

"Though I do have a rather valuable accessory I'm holding for someone else."

"I see. So that's what they're after."

I'd picked up a troublesome customer.

"I thought that if I pretended that I didn't have anything of value, then I could cut costs by getting out of needing a bodyguard."

"You idiot! I'll bill you for this later."

"All right."

He looked troubled for a minute and then nodded.

"Raphtalia, Filo. We've got trouble."

"Okay!"

"Right."

At my signal, Raphtalia jumped down from the carriage and readied herself for battle.

I pulled the accessory dealer with me and followed her out.

"You stay next to me. Got it?"

"Yes, yes!"

I switched from the shield I'd had on to unlock its ability to one that was better for combat.

"What . . . What's with your shield?"

"Oh . . ."

When the accessory dealer realized that the owner of his bird-god miracle cart was none other than the criminal Shield Hero, he looked visibly shaken.

"What's this? You're gonna fight us?"

"Sure. I didn't think it would be right to rain fire down on you from back here."

I glared the bandits down as I threatened them.

The most important thing about the fight would be preventing the enemy from getting what they were after. Basically, I couldn't let them get away with whatever the accessory dealer was carrying.

"Raphtalia, Filo, are you ready?"

"Yes. I'm ready when you are."

"Yes, I was just getting bored."

"Great. Let's do this!"

When I shouted my signal, the bandits also readied themselves and ran at us with their weapons out.

I quickly looked them over, and there seemed to be about fifteen of them. That was kind of a lot.

"Air Strike Shield!"

I aimed for one of them running at us, and the shield appeared in mid-air to halt his advance. I prepared for my next skill.

"Change Shield!"

Change Shield was a skill that would let me instantly change into any shield I needed. I chose the Bee Needle Shield. The Bee Needle Shield had a special effect of Needle Shield (small), Bee Poison (paralysis).

"The Shield! Watch out! Ugh!"

One of the running bandits collided with the shield and fell to the ground, dazed and apparently paralyzed. The skill had worked well.

"Shield Prison!"

"What?!"

The cage expanded to enclose one of the bandits.

That had a time limit on it though.

The Change Shield skill took thirty seconds to charge back up, so you couldn't use it a few times in a row. Having said that, while it did take time to recharge, it was all the more effective because of that. So it wasn't all that bad.

Suddenly three of them were right in front of me. They probably thought I looked the fool, standing there with only the shield at the ready.

I jumped in front of the merchant and covered him from an attack.

Fireworks fell away from my shield, repelled with a metallic clash. Apparently their attacks weren't strong enough to get through my defenses.

Now I had the Chimera Viper Shield out.

Its special effects were Poison Fang (medium) and Hook.

The snake engraved into the front of the shield came to life and bit at the bandits attacking me. It counter-attacked anyone that came at me and poisoned them in the process.

"Gaaahhh!"

"Dammit . . . That's it?! Ugh!!"

"I don't feel well . . ."

The Viper Shield had poisoned someone. If they'd had a resistance to poison, it wouldn't have done much.

I hadn't tried it on a person yet . . . though it seemed to be pretty powerful—not that it would take anyone down on its own.

I chose Hook next. The snake flew out from the shield and wrapped itself around someone.

It had a range of two meters, and it was useful for wrapping up an enemy (though it didn't deal any damage), pulling things closer, or climbing up cliffs or walls. I watched the bandits, and now some of them seemed so sick and unstable that they were falling over.

"This guy . . . He's the Shield Hero!"

The group of bandits suddenly appeared intimidated.

They must have just realized they'd run into me and were now starting to think back over all the various gossip they were sure to have heard. A shudder of fear rippled through the crowd, and you could see the realization cross their faces.

"Arghhhh!"

"Hiyaaaa!"

Raphtalia had her sword out, and whenever a bandit showed a weak point, she lunged at him. I had managed to fend off their attacks up until then, but they were shocked at Raphtalia's strength. One of them flew back and hit his head as he fell to the ground.

Filo was running quickly through the group and kicking at them any time she got a chance. Just like Motoyasu, they flew through the air at her kicks, five . . . no, twenty meters!

That must have killed them

Their numbers were thinning, and it seemed like there were only six of them left that were capable of standing.

Still, they were acting pompous and confident like they didn't understand the situation they were in. That they didn't retreat yet meant something . . . I was sure of it.

"Come at us already!"

"Ahhhh!"

Reinforcements rushed in. There were fifteen of them.

What a pain in the ass. They were all weak, but there were a lot of them.

And while the original group hadn't tried to surprise us, the reinforcements had.

"Heee!"

The accessory merchant let out a shrill cry, and I threw my cape open to protect him and block the arrows that had been shot at us.

Luckily, none of them were powerful enough to overcome my own high defense rating.

"There's more!"

I looked around to see a new crowd of bandits flooding from the woods toward Raphtalia.

Dammit! Where were they all coming from?

I wasn't sure anymore if we would be able to take them all down. In the worst-case scenario, we could always get back in the carriage and have Filo get us out of there . . . couldn't we?

"Ugh . . .!"

There was a loud clang, and one of the bandits had taken the full brunt of Raphtalia's sword attack . . . only to laugh it off.

What did that mean? He was a bandit but seemed much more composed than the others. He brandished the same sword as the others, but his seemed to be made from a different material.

He looked older than the others too, like a guy in his late thirties. Had he been Japanese, I'd have said that he looked like a wandering samurai. Anyway, he was wearing full, western armor, so he wasn't a samurai, but still, he looked strong.

"That's the one."

"Ha, looks like you've got the Shield Hero for a bodyguard. But I can still take him."

"Yeah."

I turned to the accessory dealer, but he quickly looked away.

"I believe that this man may have been hired to kill me."

"Heheheh . . . that one's after a class-up! I don't care if the Shield Hero is watching over him. I can still win."

Class-up? There's another thing I didn't understand.

It must have been some kind of powerful power-up, one that ordinary people couldn't use.

"We won't lose to you!"

"Raphtalia, hold off!"

"That all you got?!"

The bodyguard's sword glanced off of Raphtalia's.

Damn . . . He really was strong.

Lately Raphtalia was growing reckless. I needed to find some way to control her.

"Ah . . ."

The bodyguard grabbed Raphtalia by the chest and threatened her with his sword.

"Okay, Shield Hero, here we go. You give me that merchant, or I'll kill this girl of yours."

He was going to kill her anyway. I don't know why he had to make up this deal.

But what should I do? If he held her hostage, I couldn't even move, much less fight.

"You let her go!"

It happened in the blink of an eye. Filo ran up from behind, at full speed, and slammed into him.

"Wha . . ."

He wasn't able to get out of the way in time, but he had managed to brace himself for the impact.

When he turned his attention to Filo, he had to release Raphtalia.

But the force of Filo's impact had knocked the sword from her hand, and it clattered away. She ran to retrieve it, but in her sudden absence the bandits all turned their gaze to me.

"Die!"

"Take this!"

Clang! The shield repelled their attacks with a metallic sound.

All the attacks bounced off, except for the bodyguard. His attack had hurt.

"Hiii!"

"Don't you move!"

I was holding the accessory dealer against my side while I blocked the incoming attacks. I wasn't sure how long I was going to be able to hold out.

The guy was brushing off Raphtalia's attacks and had managed to keep his footing when Filo slammed him. How were we going to win?

I could use Shield Prison to hold him, but the skill's time limit would be a problem.

The rest of the bandits were little weaklings, so we could

pick them off one by one, but what should we do about that bodyguard?

Did it make sense to enclose him in the Shield Prison while we took care of the others? If we did, there was a chance he'd get away.

I was thinking it over when Raphtalia retrieved her sword. She was concerned about something.

What was it? Her tail was huge and bushy.

"I am the source of all power. Hear my words and understand them. Form a mirage and hide us!"

"Hide Mirage!"

Raphtalia shimmered, wavered, and then disappeared.

"She . . . She's gone!"

The bandits that had been running in her direction stopped in their tracks and appeared to be at a loss.

"Don't be a fool! She's just used magic to conceal herself."

Raphtalia's magic had improved to the point where she could use it in the middle of battle!

Damn . . . I couldn't use mine at all yet. I felt so behind!

"What the . . . Filo too?!"

Wha? Filo had crossed her arms and seemed to be concentrating.

"I am the source of all power. Hear my words and understand them. Blow them away!"

"Fast Tornado!"

A huge tornado suddenly appeared around Filo, and the nearby bandits were blown through the air.

"What?"

Even the bodyguard was surprised by all this magic, and he backed away from us to get some distance.

But he was out of luck.

Raphtalia readied her sword and approached him from behind.

"Ugh . . ."

"You were very strong, but that's why I have to do what I can to win."

She finished speaking, and the sword sliced through the back of his neck. He fell.

So we had managed to fight them off. I couldn't believe that the both of them had been able to use magic. I mean, I didn't even know that Filo COULD use magic. She should have said something. She was a monster though. Maybe it had just been instinct.

"Damn! Retreat!"

After seeing the bodyguard fall, one of the others assumed leadership and called for retreat.

"Yeah right!"

I captured that leader in a Shield Prison, and Raphtalia jumped on Filo's back to chase down the fleeing bandits.

"All right . . ."

We tied them up and looked them over.

"If we drop these guys off with the police somewhere, you think we could get an reward?"

"With how things are these days, I don't know if there is money . . ."

Raphtalia looked concerned.

"What about you? What do you know?" I asked the accessory dealer, but he shook his head.

"But you should still probably drop them off with the police."

"Yeah . . . I guess . . ."

The new leader was looking at me and laughing.

I could picture what he was thinking.

"'We were just peaceful adventurers when the Shield Hero attacked us.' Is that what you are thinking?"

He quickly stopped laughing.

"Exactly. The police would rather believe what I say than listen to you. Think of your reputation!"

"Well, you may have a point there."

Why did my reputation precede me this way? The more I thought about it, the angrier I got.

That Trash and his Bitch princess had really made me look bad, and everyone believed them.

Sigh . . .

"Fine then. We'll just have to kill you."

I hadn't given it much thought; I just said it. But the bandits had a visceral reaction. Their faces paled, and some of them began desperately working at their ropes to get free. Filo ran over and kicked them, and they fainted.

"Yeah, I've got this dangerous monster here. Might as well teach her what human tastes like."

I grit my teeth and snarled quietly and forcefully at them.

"Food?"

Filo was drooling as she looked from one bandit to the next.

"Hiiiiii?!"

"Hm . . . What to do?"

"But you're the miracle-working merchant with the bird-god carriage! You wouldn't kill someone!"

"I don't ever remember being called that. We are all responsible for our own fates. Now you all have lived by sucking off of others. Now it is your turn to pay up. Do me a favor and just accept it."

"Please! Spare our lives!"

"Fine. Give us all your valuables and equipment, and tell us where your hideout is. Go ahead and lie if you want. But I get murderous when people lie to me. And my bird-god here will tear you limb from limb. She will tear you to shreds. All I have to do is give the signal."

The bandits were shaking, and they spoke slowly, and their

voices were filled with fear. My reputation was doing me some good.

"Okay! Okay! Our hideout is . . ."

I unrolled a map and checked where they had indicated.

It was close by.

"All right. Let's negotiate."

I lowered my hand and Filo charged up a kick strong enough to knock them out. And then she delivered it.

"Take their valuables. And look how nice their equipment is! Raphtalia, that will be yours."

We had already stripped the bodyguard of his possessions. His equipment was quite good. We'd take it as payment for our troubles.

"If we steal from them, we're no better than they are."

Raphtalia protested but still followed my orders and briskly relieved the bandits of their equipment.

"All right. Now give antidote to anyone who is poisoned and load them into the carriage. Better make it quick. We still have to swing by their hideout."

"Okay!"

We went to the hideout to confirm that it really was where they had said and found someone there on watch. We tied him up and stripped him of his valuables and equipment. Then we went inside and took all the treasure and jewels they had stored and loaded them into the carriage. Finally we unloaded the tied-up bandits and left them at their hideout.

We'd gotten our hands on a large variety of treasures, like money, food, alcohol, weapons and armor, gold and silver, healing medicines, and other cheap stuff.

They'd had way more than I had been expecting, so it turned out to be more compensation than I had thought.

"That was very . . . smart."

The accessory dealer was reflecting on the event of the day and looking me over.

"Yeah . . . anyway, how much do you think our troubles on your behalf were worth?"

The merchant suddenly snapped back to reality, remembering where he was.

"Those bandits even had a bodyguard to protect them, and we defeated them all to save you. That's worth more than a few bits of silver, you know."

I gave him a little threat.

This was all his fault. I wasn't going to let him off so easily.

We agreed that I would receive one of the accessories he was selling. He said it was worth at least 20 pieces of silver.

"To be faced with such adversity and yet meet it head on! Yes, you've impressed me, Hero."

He did seem moved. He was looking at me again, more carefully than before.

I didn't think he was lying.

"Well enough. I'll give you this artifact and imbue it with magic. I will also share my business routes with you."

"That's a little much, isn't it?"

That was far more compensation than we needed, which seemed suspicious.

He might have been trying to punish us for taking one of his accessories.

"No, there aren't many merchants left like you—the kind that will demand profit even in the face of a horde of bandits."

"There must be plenty of greedy folks out there."

"That's not what I mean. Most people will wring money out of someone and then toss them aside, but not you. You know how to keep them alive so that you can continue to profit from them."

"Keep them alive for profit . . ."

I looked over at the tied-up bandits.

They might have been a powerful group of bandits, but here they were tied up. Their clothes and equipment were all very nice, and they had evidently stolen it all from others. If we were to steal all of it back from them, what was wrong with that? Don't they say that you reap what you sow?

"You mean because of all this?"

"Those men came after us to steal our money and our lives. But you compromised and took all their possessions but left them their lives. Normally you'd have to kill them. If you think about it, this is the best ending they could hope for."

I did have a really bad reputation, so there really was a

chance that the police would have taken the word of bandits over my own. Then again, they might have believed me.

"They paid for their lives with all their material possessions."

"You could put that way . . ."

"And once they build up their loot again and come for revenge, you'll beat them and take it all again!"

The accessory dealer flashed a wicked smile.

What was with this guy? He was starting to freak me out!

"Anyway, we'll drop you off at the next town."

"No thanks. I have so much to tell you. I won't leave until I've shared it all with you."

He thought I was his apprentice or something!

Something was off-putting about all this. What was he up to?

Anyway, we warmed our pockets and wallets with the bandit's stash and set out on the road again.

This might not be immediately relevant, but apparently there was a merchant's guild, and a corrupt member of it had sold the bandits the information that this accessory dealer had gotten a ride in our carriage. That guy was later removed from the guild.

Chapter Fourteen: Magic Practice

For whatever reason, the accessory dealer insisted on riding with us from that point on.

He was paying us for the trouble, so I couldn't think of anything to complain about. Still, I didn't know why he wanted to come with us.

After the incident with the bandits he apparently had grown fond of me, and he started to reveal things about himself, and he took to lecturing me on various topics when we were on the road.

Anyway, he said that there were traveling merchants messing up trade in the area and that the merchants guild sent him out to keep an eye on things. Basically, the guy was one of the guild's assassins.

And he had seen potential in me and wanted to see how I developed. Furthermore, this guy was apparently a pretty powerful member of the guild, though afterward I heard from other members of that guild that he wasn't well known for sharing and teaching others.

The first thing he started talking about was how to procure the materials you would need to imbue jewels and things with power. One of his acquaintances was able to help us with that.

Next, he spoke about how to form precious metals into accessories. Apparently you could choose from a number of different designs. I have always been a bit of an *Otaku*, so I picked a design that sort of fit my sensibilities. It turned out a little differently than intended, but I still liked it.

We were also able to get tools necessary for the process, and we got them cheaply.

Some of the tools didn't exist back in my world, such as a material for burning like coal. It was called a magic stone.

The shield started to respond to it, but the material was too expensive to just let the shield absorb it.

There were things that, back in my world, would have been called grinders. There were also things like burners, too. They were used to form the accessory.

Iron and other hard materials could be brought to a forge where metal molds could be used to form smaller items. Anyway, my crafting skill made the process a bit easier than it would have been otherwise.

There were other tools that were needed for making higher-level items, but they were too expensive to think about buying now. That's how our finances were looking.

That brings me to the main problem: how to imbue something with magic.

If you couldn't use magic, you couldn't do it.

I couldn't use magic yet, so I was sitting there with the

book in one hand, muttering along, when the accessory dealer started talking again.

"Hero, are you unable to use magic?"

"That's right. I've asked my helpers here how they do it, but they just say to 'synchronize with my spirit.' I don't know what they are talking about."

"Ah . . . yes, I think I am beginning to understand."

The accessory dealer reached into his pocket and pulled out a small, translucent piece of something.

"What's this?"

"It's a piece of very valuable ore."

"Huh . . ."

"Can you read?"

"A little . . . if it's simple."

I'd been studying the writing for about a month now, and if I focused hard enough, I could read it. If it was very complicated, then I couldn't follow it, but if it was simple enough, I could.

"Then let's work on your magic practice. If you can learn to feel the power, that's enough."

Ugh . . . This sounded like torture to me.

I was worried about the prospect of study, but I reached out my hand and took the shard of ore. It began to glow.

What . . . What did it mean? It was like . . . like feeling a hand move that you didn't know you had—yes, it was like that.

Or it was how a bird must have felt when it opens its wings for the first time and flew.

"Something feels weird."

"You can actually feel your magical power without the aid of that stone, but you were raised without knowing that. I thought it might help you, so I handed it over. Turns out it was a good choice."

"I guess so."

I thought back to a concept I had translated from the magic book and began to recite it.

I imagined magic as another arm, and then I tried to imagine that that other arm was MY arm.

Some words appeared. It was only for me—my own, private magic.

"I am the source of all power. Hear my words and understand them. Protect them!"

"Fast Guard!"

I became aware of a target marker blinking in my field of vision. I chose myself as the target to practice the spell.

I was suddenly covered in a soft light.

I checked my status screen to see that my defense had risen dramatically.

"Whoa . . ."

"Looks like you were able to figure it out. Now allow me to show you how to imbue an object with magic."

The accessory dealer ignored my impressed reaction and immediately moved into his lecture.

It had been a big step for me, but apparently he wasn't impressed.

I listened to his lecture, and pretty soon I had learned how to imbue an object with magic.

I tried imbuing the jewel that we'd made with magic, which involved controlling the natural tendencies of the stone.

It was a little difficult at first, but I could use magic now, and the skills from the shield were helping. Eventually I was able to produce a few pieces. Apparently there were more advanced techniques, like using different stones and mixing their properties or absorbing the magic from different plants and then imbuing other objects with that magic.

"Well, that's the gist of it. I think you can figure out the rest by yourself. I hope it helps you and your business."

The accessory dealer gave a final farewell and then climbed down from the carriage.

Now I had another skill besides compounding—I could craft magical jewels.

We would need different ores to use in the crafting, so we visited the mining town we'd stopped by earlier.

"Ah . . . so he sent you here, did he?"

A large man, a miner, was looking me over suspiciously, but I showed him the letter of introduction the accessory dealer had given us.

"Yeah, that's his handwriting. But to think you'd be introduced by him? He's very strict about money."

"What's that supposed to mean?"

I listened to the miner's gossip. Apparently the accessory dealer was well known as a miser.

He'd thought it suspicious that a guy like that would introduce me, but he accepted it once he saw the letter.

"Well, if he sent you here, then sure, you can buy from me. How much are you looking for? I think I can accommodate you."

"You think I could go mine them out myself? That should help keep costs down, right?"

"Huh? Oh, well . . . If you want to do it yourself, then it would basically be free, but . . ."

We talked it over, and before long, Filo, Raphtalia, and I were down in a cave with pickaxes in our hands. The rhythmic clanging of our pickaxes echoed in the silent cave. Honestly, it was a real racket.

The air was so stuffy and hot I couldn't stand it.

The walls rippled with glowing veins of ore—much different from the last mine we'd been in.

"This is a pretty safe and stable cavern, so you should be fine to dig and mine anywhere you want. Having said that, there is always a chance of a cave-in or of falling rocks, so do be careful."

That only made sense.

From the way he made it sound, there were a number of caves, but he had led us to the richest one.

I raised my pickax and brought it down against the stone wall. When I did, a glowing cross appeared on the wall.

It was just like when we were looking for Light Metal.

"Hiya!"

I swung the pickax with all my might.

The impact echoed in the cavern, and the wall cracked. The crack slowly expanded and creaked, and the wall fell apart.

"Huh?"

The miner was staring at me, wide-eyed.

"You broke through that hard stone with one hit?"

Was it so hard?

Thanks to my collection skill, I was able to break through the rocks easily, and pretty soon there were piles of ore rolling out from the cracks. And yet, no doubt because of my level, I still came upon walls that I couldn't break into, no matter how severe my effort.

"Please take this."

"Oh, okay."

We stuffed the ore into a bag and hurried from the mine.

By the way, even outside the mine itself, we were able to find ore pretty much anywhere we swung our pickaxes. Apparently it was really easy to find in the area.

The only problem was that any ore found near the surface tended to be of poor magical quality.

Back in my world, I think I had heard that if you find a place rich in ore, it would be everywhere and easy to take too. Maybe things were different here and good ore was somehow a function of its depth below the surface.

You made a Ruby Bracelet!
Ruby Bracelet: quality: good to excellent

I tried out my new skills and, I guess because the original materials were good, ended up with something very nice.

Now it was time to try imbuing it with magic.

Ruby Bracelet (fire resistance up): quality: excellent to normal

Damn . . . I was able to imbue it with magic, but I lowered the quality rating in the process.

We went on with our travels, and I tried crafting different accessories in the back of the carriage.

You know, crafting in the back of a moving carriage is not an easy thing to do. When I thought about how long it took compared to the relative ease of compounding medicines, I wasn't sure if it was any more profitable. And on top of that, I let the shield absorb both finished pieces and raw materials but was never able to unlock anything. Apparently my level and tree were not advanced enough.

I'd have to focus on sales.

By the way, that bracelet that I made sold after only two days for 80 pieces of silver. But it took a long time to make the base of the bracelet.

And it seemed like jewels were less valuable in this world than they were in mine.

I wondered if the design of the accessory, and how in-line it was with the current fashion trends, would affect the price I could get for it. Would its design affect its price? The very idea struck me as ironic.

But apparently they were in the midst of a popularity boom, and apparently there were fashionable trends in this world too.

I guess I just didn't know what jewels could be sold for a good price. Even still—I was making money. Pretty soon it would be time to buy all new equipment.

Iron Ore Shield: conditions met
Copper Ore Shield: conditions met
Silver Ore Shield: conditions met
Lead Ore Shield: conditions met

Iron Ore Shield: ability locked: equip bonus: metalworking skill 2

Copper Ore Shield: ability locked: equip bonus: metalworking skill 1

Silver Ore Shield: ability locked: equip bonus: damage from demonic monsters reduced by 2%

Lead Ore Shield: ability locked: equip bonus: defense 1

I was unlocking a bunch of abilities that seemed better left in the hands of the guy from the weapon shop. It didn't make sense to try and do EVERYTHING on my own.

The Lead Ore Shield seemed to be taking the place of something else.

I don't think that skill will see much use.

We had been traveling like that for a few days when we arrived at a town in the south. That's when it happened.

The accessory dealer had told us that there was an area that was desperately in need of large quantities of weed killer.

We'd have to travel quickly to reach them in time, but that's what the bird-god . . . That's what Filo was for.

If we stood to make a lot of money, then there was nothing to debate. We hurried to the southwest.

Chapter Fifteen: Why It Was Sealed

So there was a village that needed a large quantity of weed killer. We hurried there.

"Master!"

"What is it?"

"Um . . . These plants are amazing!"

Raphtalia and I craned our necks to look outside. The street was covered in writhing vines so thick they threatened to cover the entire street.

"What the hell?!"

It was moving slowly, but if you watched closely you could see the vines crawling out further and spreading over the road.

"The village . . ."

I looked around to get a sense of our surroundings, and I saw something in the distance that looked something like a refugee camp.

"Filo, take us over there."

"Okay."

We arrived at the camp and quickly started selling our products.

"All right, so what price should we set for the weed killer?"

They must have needed it to try and control those vines we'd seen.

I was starting to understand why the accessory dealer recommended this place to us—sure enough, we should be able to do some business here.

But how much? How much money would we make off with?

"There might be a specialized buyer."

"Good point."

We climbed out of the carriage and started asking around.

I changed my shield into the Book Shield. Then I rotated it around to the inside of my arm and pretended to be a merchant just walking around with his book. If they didn't notice my shield, they wouldn't think I was the Shield Hero.

"I heard that you were in need of weed killer and were willing to pay for it."

I found someone in the camp dressed better than the others. He seemed to be in charge.

"Ah . . . A merchant? You're just in time."

"What happened here?"

I looked off in the distance to see the whole area covered in vines.

"Yes, well . . . Our village was experiencing a severe famine."

That reminded me . . . I think I'd heard about this place. But didn't Motoyasu take care of it?

"The Spear Hero was able to release the seal on an ancient miracle seed for us. That solved the famine, and yet . . ."

"You mean this is from the miracle seed?"

I looked back at the vines. Looking closely, I saw various fruits and vegetables growing from the twisting stalks.

So the refugees had plenty to eat, and the famine was solved. They were able to get potatoes from the roots. They were digging at the vines with shovels.

So apparently they were able to fix the famine problem, but the vines were too powerful, and they ran out of space to live?

How stupid can you get?

Thinking back on it, that must have been the reason the seed was sealed away in the first place. If they had just left it there, everything would have been fine.

Motoyasu, the fool! What was he thinking?

Oh yeah . . . We'd been nearby a little while ago when we were with the witch.

"To he who would break the seal of the seed. It is my desire that this seed never be released into the world. It will play with the people's desire to be freed from famine, granting their wish in the worst way imaginable. The seal is not so easily broken."

Yeah, that's what it had said. Why would he break the seal on the seed?

He must not have read it. He must not have known that from all his game experience.

"Out here on the periphery there is no major problem. But if you head into the village, the plants have begun to turn into monsters."

So the plants could mutate . . . Great.

He really was an idiot.

It was so easy to put me in a bad mood. It had happened so quickly this time.

He was very skilled. He knew how to ruin my mood.

"So that's why you want weed killer?"

"Yes."

If these people were farmers, you'd think they already knew how to control weeds . . . but whatever.

"At first we were all so happy. But once the vines came over our fields and then our houses . . . Well, we went out with axes to try and hold the vines at bay, but they were too fast."

"When did all this happen?"

"Once the hero moved on, we didn't have any trouble for two weeks. But about half a month ago, things started to . . ."

"Uh huh. Didn't you report to the Crown?"

"Yes. But they said that it would take a while before a hero would be able to make it out here. Therefore, we have been forced to do what we can with weed killer for the time being . . ."

Huff . . . I let out an involuntary sigh.

"Why don't you try burning it?"

"We've tried everything that we could think of."

"So I guess you tried burning it . . ."

They had probably tried reaching out to adventurers for help too.

I looked around the camp, and sure enough, there were a bunch of people with weapons and equipment there. They would not be villagers.

"Ahhhhhhhhhhh!"

An ear-splitting shriek came from the direction of the village.

"What was that?!"

"We tried to stop him, but there was an adventurer that wanted to fight in the village to raise his levels. That must be him."

The villager sighed his answer, as though he'd done all he could.

"Damn! Filo!"

"Okay!"

I pointed in the direction of the village. Filo had been stuffing her cheeks with fruit from the vines but immediately took off running at my signal.

She ran, full speed, right into the village and came back shortly with three adventurers. They were beaten up pretty badly.

"How did the village look?"

"Hmm . . . Well, the monster plants were wriggling over everything. There were some cool ones that spit poison and acid and stuff. Weak adventurers shouldn't go in there! Stupid!"

"That last part wasn't necessary."

"Okay!"

The villagers were shocked when they saw Filo talking.

"Oh, we've heard of you! You're the miracle-working saint with the bird-god carriage!"

As if they just noticed me, they ran over and shook my hand.

"Well I don't know about saint . . . but I have a bird and a carriage."

"Please save our village! There are people even that have been consumed by the vines!"

"You mean they are parasitic? Oh jeez . . ."

I took some restorative medicine and some weed killer and then was led over to a tent. Inside there were a number of people lying down, and their bodies were half-transformed into plants.

"I can't promise that I can cure them. And besides, I'm no philanthropist. I expect to be paid."

"Yes . . ."

I went over to the closest patient, a child that seemed to be having trouble breathing, and administered the restorative medicine.

The child was enveloped in a soft light, and his breathing seemed to stabilize. I then applied weed killer to the affected areas of his body.

The child was in pain for a short time, but then the leaves withered and fell off, and the child seemed to be cured.

"Oh . . ."

"That's a saint for you!"

Everyone was whispering in amazement. I administered the same medicine routine to the remaining patients.

Once everyone had been treated, the atmosphere around the camp improved greatly. I guess anyone would be happy to see their lot improve, however little.

"Thank you! Thank you so much!"

Everyone thanked me.

"Time to pay up."

I asked for a price that was higher than the average market price.

Here's why: if they had already appealed to the Crown for help, then there was a chance that another hero might show up at any time. And if he did, then pretty soon they would know who I was too, and then they'd be singing a different tune.

The villagers happily paid me. Everything was going according to plan.

"All right, I'll sell you the weed killer. Let's try to make this quick. Once you buy it, I'm out of here."

"Um . . . Saint . . . Could you please save our village?"

"What?! I thought you'd asked for a hero to come."

"Yes, but . . ."

Ugh . . . All the villagers were throwing themselves at my feet and begging me.

I wasn't exactly all-powerful here. And besides, it's not like I had any responsibility to them.

"No thanks."

"Please. If you need money, we'll find a way . . ."

"You need to pay upfront. And if anything happens, I don't want to hear any complaints. Now, if you know anything about the seed that the Spear Hero unsealed, you better tell me about it now."

The villagers called out to one another, and soon I was surrounded by people pulling money from their pockets. I spent the time trying to find out all that I could.

Apparently the seed had been sealed away in some nearby ruins and had been watched over by a powerful guardian.

If the vines were overtaking everything, someone must have wondered what had happened to the guardian. No? I sighed . . . These villagers weren't good for much.

The villagers believed that the seed was the masterwork of an alchemist that had made his hideaway in those ruins and that the seed was sealed away sometime later on. According to reports that they had, the area had, sometime in the past, been overtaken by vines.

"If you have a legend like that around here, why would you remove the seal from the seed? Didn't anyone notice?"

Everyone turned their eyes to the ground.

They must have thought it was safe because a hero had brought it to them.

We were talking all this over when they announced they had raised the money I'd requested.

It was quite a lot of money. I could have taken it and just run off.

"Okay, I've got it. I'll do what I can."

I changed my shield to the Chimera Viper Shield. That would be better for battle.

"Sh . . . The Shield Hero?!"

I ignored the shouts of the villagers and pressed on farther into the vines. Raphtalia and Filo followed close behind.

I put all the money into a pouch and tied it around my waist, then moved deeper and deeper into the vines.

Chapter Sixteen: Invading Vines

"Raphtalia, Filo, be careful."

Okay, so we'd be fighting plants today.

I'd gotten used to handling herbs and grasses, but the plants surrounding us now were completely different.

The vines were covered with different fruits, and the roots were studded with potatoes. That wasn't all. They were parasitic (and could infect your body) and could spit poison and acid.

I was thinking that the weed killer was probably our best bet. Physically, though, I didn't know if cutting them or beating them in battle would really do much.

We walked for a little while before the wriggling vines decided to attack us.

"Hah!"

"Hiyah!"

Raphtalia and Filo took care of them quickly.

But it didn't do anything to stop the vines. If anything, it caused more trouble, as now the other vines were taking an interest in us.

We could try using magic . . .

"I am the source of all power. Hear my words and understand them. Protect them!"

"Fast Guard!"

I cast a protective spell on Raphtalia and Filo.

The spell would raise the defense rating of the target. If I used it on myself it was even more effective, because my defense was already so high.

"Thank you, Mr. Naofumi."

"Thanks!"

They both thanked me, but we were soon attacked by other vines again.

We could have kept pressing on, but what did we need to do to get rid of the vines for good?

Without weed killer or magic we'd have no choice but to retreat. But as things stood now, maybe we could just kill them one by one and move on.

If we met the monsters in the heart of the village, they might have a hint or two that we could use.

We didn't know how they had broken through the seal, so I didn't have any concrete ideas. So all we could do was try what we could until we found something that worked.

In a worst-case scenario, we'd have to go back to those ruins—and that would be a pain.

The vines weren't strong enough to get through my defenses, so they weren't able to do much to halt our progress.

"Keep going! We'll figure it out when we get there."

"Okay!"

We ran on and came to what seemed to be the origin of the vine's roots, at the very center.

The whole area was crawling with plant-based monsters. They weren't so strong that Raphtalia and Filo couldn't take care of them. Even still, I wanted to make sure that they were protected.

"Um . . ."

The monsters' names were BioPlant, PlantRiwe, and Mandragora.

BioPlant referred to some kind of master-plant from which all the other enemies were produced. PlantRiwe referred specifically to a human-shaped amalgamation of different vines. The Mandragora was like a large, immobile pitcher plant.

The poison-spitting monster that Filo had mentioned was the Mandragora. The PlantRiwe had a giant flower growing from its head, and the flower released clouds of poisonous pollen. The Mandragora produced an acidic liquid from its vines, which it would fling at weaker creatures and then, once stunned, would pull them into its gaping mouth.

The BioPlant was the real monster, as the other two were produced by it. The vine would form a bulbous growth that would get larger and larger until it burst, producing the other monsters.

I tried sprinkling it with weed killer, and it reacted instantly, withering and dying as if I'd stabbed it through its heart.

That didn't seem to break my nonaggression rule (the one imposed by the shield), I guess because the beasts were really more like plants than monsters.

I wonder how this shield was making its judgment.

I bet it was like that . . . like when you could use holy water on an undead monster to knock it out. It must have been based on the original use intended by the object. Either that or it was because the medicine was designed to return the plants to their parasitic form.

Whatever, I don't know.

"What happened?"

The PlantRiwe and Mandragoras kept on uselessly attacking me.

Their attacks weren't doing anything, but the poisonous pollen was starting to affect my breath. And the acid was getting annoying too. Both of them had the effect of lowering a target's defense rating, and when I checked my status screen I could tell that it was having an effect on me.

Still, they weren't able to hurt me, so that was good. Unfortunately the Snake Poison Fang (medium) wasn't having any effect on them.

I suppose I should have expected that. The monsters used poison too, and they were plants.

"Raphtalia!"

"Cough! What is it?"

The air was very thick, and by the look of it Raphtalia was having trouble breathing.

Even though I had managed to heal her in the past, her respiratory system was probably still damaged and weaker than everyone else's.

"Here! You take some weed killer too."

"Oh, okay!"

I tossed her a bottle of weed killer. I'd have her use it in case there was an emergency or something.

The vines wriggled toward her and tried to attack her, but Raphtalia calmly stepped back and sliced through them.

They weren't nearly as durable as I'd expected.

"Mr. Naofumi? I'm going!"

"Oh . . . um."

We pressed on until we came to the town square. There was a large tree growing there.

Actually no . . . It wasn't a tree. It was a bunch of vines all twisted together.

"That's the source! I hope . . ."

We approached the trunk of the "tree," and suddenly a giant eye appeared from it and stared at us.

"!!!!!!!!!!!!!!!!!!!!!!!!!!!!"

That was creepy. But it did seem to be the source.

"Master! I'm going!"

Filo took off running in the direction of the tree, but vines extended from it to meet her.

"Yaaaah!"

She drew back her powerful leg and kicked the vines, sending them flying through the air before jumping to her feet and turning to face the tree. Realization flashed over her face: she was still too far away.

"Master!"

"I know! Air Strike Shield!"

Filo was falling through the air, but the Air Strike Shield deployed right under her, and she landed on it.

She caught her footing on the floating shield before jumping off again and landing directly before the giant eye.

"Hiyah!"

There was a nasty sound of gushing liquid, and the eye exploded at Filo's powerful kick.

Ugh . . . It was pretty nasty.

"!!!!!!!!!!!!!!!!!!!!!!!!!!!!!!!!!!!!"

The tree of vines began to violently writhe. Apparently taking out its eye wasn't enough to kill it.

What should we do?

"It's not falling!"

"I know."

With an awful wriggling and gush, the eye reappeared.

In the process, just for a second, I could see something like a seed deep within the eye.

"Raphtalia, Filo, I just saw something inside the eye there.

Try dumping weed killer on it."

My skill was done with its necessary cool down time. I sent out another Air Strike Shield. I should point out that I was being attacked this whole time by PlantRiwes and Mandragoras. They kept raining down from above from some inexhaustible supply.

"Okay!"

"Got it!"

Raphtalia jumped on Filo's back and they ran for the rapidly regenerating eyeball.

The eye, probably noticing the threat, sent vines shooting straight for them. Even more streamed down from above.

"Shield Prison!"

A cage immediately appeared and enclosed Raphtalia and Filo. They were suspended in the cage in mid-air, but they should be able to make their attack from that spot.

The skill would only last for fifteen seconds.

During that time, all the vines streaming down from above bounced back from the cage.

But no . . . Now they were winding around the bars.

Fifteen seconds had passed, and the cage vanished. At the same time, to support them, I released an Air Strike Shield to catch Filo where she fell.

"Hiyah!"

Filo caught her footing on the shield and Raphtalia flashed

her sword at the swarming vines.

It looked like she was successful as all the vines fell back. Filo was successful again, and she ran to make another approach.

She managed to land another successful kick on the eyeball.

"!???????"

The regenerating eye completely stopped moving after taking Filo's second kick.

Finding her window of opportunity, Raphtalia leaned over and poured the weed killer on the small seed-like object.

"!!!!?????"

There was an unbelievable loud shriek followed by violent writhing. Then all the BioPlants stopped moving.

"Did it work?"

It sure seemed to have worked, and I hadn't been hurt at all in the process.

But then the BioPlants all started to move again.

"I'm sorry. I guess I didn't do it right!"

"You did fine. I guess it just wasn't strong enough . . ."

But now what were we supposed to do?

But wait . . . I had an idea.

I had a skill that increased medicine efficacy. Wasn't that how I was able to help all those people?

Did that mean that . . . that I should be the one to use the weed killer?

"Let me try. I think I can do it."

I held a bottle in my hand and stalked off for the eye.

I had just started to notice it recently, but my defense rating completely negated the attacks of my enemies. Even if I was covered with them I could still walk just fine. But once I tried attacking, the power balance wasn't so clear-cut.

There was a BioPlant in front of me, its roots exposed from the soil.

"I guess I really should ride on Filo to get close to that seed . . ."

But I poured the weed killer on the roots of the BioPlant.

"!!!!!!!!!!!!!!!!!!!!!!!!!!!!!!!!!!?????????????????"

The plants were writhing very quickly and violently. They were screaming like monsters.

The eye turned brown, and the rot spread out from the eye to cover the rest of the creature.

Suddenly the entire plant began to dry up.

There was a cracking sound as the tree dried and wilted, then suddenly crumbled. We had to run to escape the falling pieces.

"Whoa . . ."

We looked around to find all the plant monsters brown and wilted. Everything but the fruit had turned brown, and we were the only things moving.

And then . . . from where the BioPlant tree had stood, a great number of glowing seeds rained down from above.

Leaving them there seemed like a bad idea.

"Now it's cleanup time. I might be able to absorb some into my shield. Let's start collecting seeds."

"Okay."

"Lunch time!"

Filo watched Raphtalia and I collect seeds while she feasted on the leftover fruits and potatoes.

Chapter Seventeen: Improving the Product Line

"Is that it?"

"Yeah, we'll leave the rest up to the villagers."

The miracle seed . . . We'd dispatched with the BioPlants that Motoyasu had woken up . . . and now we were collecting seeds.

We had fistfuls of seeds, and I went ahead and let the shield absorb the wilted plants as we worked.

BioPlant Shield: conditions met
PlantRiwe Shield: conditions met
Mandragora Shield: conditions met

BioPlant Shield: ability locked: equip bonus: plant reform
Special Effect: Hook
PlantRiwe Shield: ability locked: equip bonus: intermediate compounding recipes 2
Mandragora Shield: ability locked: equip bonus: plant analysis

The plant-type shield unlocked a tree that connected to the others. It looked like there were other things I could access as well, but the tree hadn't advanced enough.

"Plant Reform?"

I'd received an interesting-looking ability from the BioPlant, but I'd have to experiment a little to see how it worked.

An icon appeared that indicated I should select a seed to imbue with magic.

I decided to try it on one of the BioPlant seeds that I had just picked up.

The seed slowly rose and floated in the air.

Special Abilities: propagation 9, production 9, vitality 9, immunity 4, intelligence 1, growth 9, mutation 9

What was this all about? I decided to put the seed down.

There was a quick series of beeps, and the numbers fell quickly. Hm . . . I didn't understand.

I decided to try lowering some stats and raising just one.

Special Abilities: propagation 1, production 1, vitality1, immunity 1, intelligence 1, growth 43, mutation 1

Oh, okay, so I just had to focus on raising the growth stat.

Oh, hey now—when I used the skill, my magic power dropped dramatically.

"Mr. Naofumi?"

I dropped the modified BioPlant seed on a dry patch of ground nearby.

"Whoa!"

Nearly instantaneously, the ground was split and covered in green vines.

But . . .

"Huh?"

The plant grew to be about three meters in size before suddenly drying up.

"What are you doing?"

"I got this new ability, Plant Reform, and I wanted to try it out on this seed here."

"You shouldn't do such dangerous things!"

Raphtalia was upset with me. Whatever. Had I watched someone do what I'd done, I'd probably have been angry too.

But what an ability it was! If I gave serious thought to it, I could probably make a real miracle seed.

"Mr. Naofumi . . . that's a weird smile on your face."

Damn . . . she'd found me out.

"Anyway, let's head back to the village."

"Okay."

We turned our backs on the newly silent, brown land and made for the camp.

"Thank you so much, Hero!"

People were all about cash. After I saved their village, here they were, waving to me.

Still, the village would take a lot of cleaning before it was livable again. It would be a lot of work. We spent the rest of the day disposing of the wilted plants.

The main body of the plants had wilted away, but the fruits and potatoes they'd produced seemed just fine. They would have food for a while here.

But I was a little worried about the soil. Had the plants sucked all the nutrients from it?

"Well, this is the opposite of a famine, isn't it?"

"I suppose so, yes."

In the near future, this village might need to pack up and move on.

I was thinking it over, and it inspired me to look deeper into this Plant Reform ability. I still didn't know what it meant by "special ability."

I tried to look it up, and an icon appeared saying that I needed the plant analysis ability.

That had been part of the Mandragora Shield, so I would have to wait for the ability to unlock.

I actually thought that the Mandragora Shield abilities would unlock faster, so I switched my shield to the Mandragora Shield before I went to bed. When I woke up the next morning, the ability had been unlocked, so I switched back to the BioPlant Shield and tried my hand at plant reformation again.

Special Abilities: propagation 9, production 9, vitality 9, immunity 4, intelligence 1, growth 9, mutation 9
Dried Seed Growth: mutation range expansion

I was starting to get it . . . This must have been the abilities of the BioPlant.

It must have meant that the seed was developed to produce a lot of food, but its mutation rating was so high that it got out of control.

To think, the old alchemist had gone out of his way to leave that message of warning too . . . He couldn't have been all bad.

And the immunity rating was low, which must be why the weed killer had been effective.

I looked for the special ability icon, and when I selected it, a number of different options appeared, along with a few special messages. It was possible to sacrifice or augment different attributes.

It would be a real shame if the village had to return to its days of famine.

So I decided to experiment a little.

Propagation . . . 4. This was simple. It was just how quickly the plant spread. It seemed too high, so I lowered it.

Production . . . 15. This, no doubt, controlled how much food the plant produced. It should be high enough to solve the famine.

Vitality . . . 6. This would help the plant grow in any type of soil. I lowered it a little.

Immunity . . . 4. This was how the plant fought off disease. At the current level, weed killer worked fine. So I left it where it was.

Intelligence . . . 1. What was this supposed to be? A monster's intelligence? Why would you want to raise this?

Growth . . . 15. This was how quickly the plant would grow once planted. I raised the level.

Mutation . . . 1. This must have been what turned the plants into monsters.

Special Abilities: I unchecked the box that would expand the range of mutation and decided to add the ability of quality improvement.

Dried Seed Growth: quality improvement

"There. I'm done."

"What did you do?"

Raphtalia was fighting off a yawn when she replied to me.

"Oh, I'm just working a bit more on that thing from yesterday."

"You're still working on that?"

"Well, we can't just leave things the way that they are."

If we did, the famine would just come back. So we had to do something to stop it. I thought about going to another village and buying food for the place, but there were too many people living here to make that a viable option. It would be hard to get them to pack up and move . . . considering how settled they were here.

"Okay then . . ."

I climbed down from the carriage and dropped the seed into some dry soil.

It happened so quickly. A large plant emerged from the seed and covered a portion of the wilted, brown village.

"What the hell is going on?!"

Villagers that had been resting came over to us in shock.

"Oh, yeah—sorry. I'm just experimenting a little."

"What are you doing?"

They must have been afraid of the plants, because their voices wavered as they asked.

"I'm trying to turn this into a safe version of what it was."

I'd set the propagation level low, so once the plant reached its size it wouldn't spread beyond a certain range.

And then . . .

Red, juicy, tomato-like fruits popped into view all over the vine. The majority of the fruits looked just like tomatoes.

"Looks like I was successful."

"Whoa . . ."

"The main problem is that's really only making one kind of fruit now. It's up to you whether or not you want to use it. But if you don't want it, then make sure you to take care of it before things get out of control."

So the mutation and mutation range expansion were the real problems . . . They allowed you to grow a lot of different kinds of fruit but at the risk of the plants turning into monsters.

I sprinkled weed killer over the plant and it returned to a seed. I picked it up and gave it to a man who seemed to be the governor.

"All right, we're out of here. Later."

Filo woke up and stuffed her cheeks with the remaining tomatoes before taking her place at the front of the carriage.

"Wait just a minute!"

"Huh? What?"

"We haven't shown our gratitude yet, so please take this . . ."

"Those idiots . . . They just tried to pass their excess onto me. Didn't they?"

"I . . . I don't know."

Our carriage was now three cars long.

Filo pulled the front carriage, but now we had two additional carts hooked to the back that were loaded down with fruits and vegetables from the BioPlant.

They'd given us the carts and the food, probably because it would have all rotted if they didn't get rid of it. They just passed it off on me and even had the gall to ask me to come back anytime.

Their faces were beaming when they gave it all to me, so I wasn't going to refuse it. Even still, I couldn't help but feel that they were just foisting their problems off on me. Oh, and by the way, even though we were three full carts now, Filo had no problem at all pulling us.

"It's so heavy. I love it!"

Filolials sure were weird monsters.

Our carriage rattled down the idyllic road, and our journey went on.

But this all had me thinking. I could use this weed killer as a weapon, right? If so, I was determined to try it on any Torrents that we came across.

But when I got my chance, it didn't work at all.

Apparently it would only work on plants that had parasitic tendencies.

These rules were seeming more random by the minute.

Maybe the BioPlant wasn't really a monster at all but just a plant.

Whatever, it didn't matter. With how strong Filo and Raphtalia were getting, I didn't need to worry about attacking by myself.

The first thing we needed to do was figure out a way to get rid of all this food. The last thing I wanted was it rotting on me. But hey—Filo was chomping it down so quickly . . . maybe it wouldn't be an issue at all.

"Where should we go next?"

We were talking it over and trying to figure out where we should go next when we started to hear rumors about a land to the east that was having problems with some kind of infectious disease.

So we decided to make a bunch of medicine and head in that direction.

"All right, we're going east!"

"Okay!"

Chapter Eighteen: Diseased Village

We ended up camping that night.

We had left all the food just sitting in the carts, but Filo seemed to be having her way with it, so we'd just leave it like that for a while.

During the time we had spent on the road, we heard rumors of another famine in the north. We decided to take a detour to the southwest to pick up more food. They would have trouble keeping it anyway, and we could probably sell it for a good price.

"I'm hungry!"

Filo stuck her head under the tarp we'd covered the carts with and started fishing around for food.

"Oh, yummmmmmmmmies!"

I'd heard that before.

Filo had finished with her growth spurt but still ate a ton of food. The amount she went through every day was pretty unbelievable. She paid for it by pulling us all down the road at a brisk pace. It was almost too brisk, really. We had to stop and make repairs to the carts relatively frequently.

"What happened?"

I thought about changing out the wooden parts for metal ones. Filo was always complaining about how light things were.

But thinking about the improved durability made me wonder just how much it would end up costing.

Raphtalia had started to get over her motion sickness, but Filo ran over all the dips and jumps in the road so quickly that most of our passengers ended up puking. We should probably add springs or something to the axels, something to cushion all the shocks.

We'd made quite a lot of money recently. I was looking forward to visiting the weapon shop.

After spending some time wandering around the country, I could now say with certainty that that old guy had the best weapon shop in the whole kingdom.

I didn't know where the other heroes were getting their equipment, but in all of my travels I had yet to come across even one shop that was as good as his was.

"Master!"

Ugh . . . Filo ran over and leaned on me with her heavy wings.

"Ehehehe."

"Ugh . . ."

Raphtalia, for some reason, sidled up close to me.

"He, he, he . . . We're all so warm and cuddly."

"I'm hot, actually."

"Filo, you back away. If you back off, then we'll be super comfortable."

"No! Raphtalia should back away! You can't just keep Master all to yourself."

"I'm not keeping him all to myself!"

"Both of you go the hell to sleep!"

"But . . ."

"But we should sleep together! Masterrrrrr!"

I went over our stocks of medicine and soon realized that we were not going to have enough. I quickly began working to make more. It bothered me that there was no way to know whether or not I'd made enough . . . but I guess that's just part of the job.

"Bu . . ."

Filo sulked and dragged her feet as she went outside.

At the same time, Raphtalia climbed into the carriage. I guess it beat sleeping on the hard ground.

"All right."

It was my turn to watch the fire, so I sat down and started working on my compounding.

"Mr. Naofumi."

"Huh?"

I turned to look at the carriage. Raphtalia was there in the back, motioning for me to come over.

"What is it?"

"Let's sleep together."

"Not you too! You two sure are needy. Did you have a bad dream or something?"

She used to have such bad dreams that she couldn't sleep without someone there next to her.

Granted, she had good reasons for having bad dreams, considering how she'd lost her parents and all that.

"I did not!"

She protested. But no matter how much she might look like an adult, she was still a kid on the inside. She must have wanted a parental figure.

"That's not it? You should get Filo to turn into a girl. Then you can sleep with her if you are lonely."

"It's not that I'm lonely, exactly."

Raphtalia, suddenly embarrassed, turned her eyes to the floor.

That reminds me. Just when did she stop crying in the night? It felt like a very long time ago.

"Mr. Naofumi . . . Back in your own world . . . Was there anyone you . . . liked?"

"Huh? No."

What the hell was she talking about? I had no idea what she wanted.

"What's up with you?"

"Nothing. I . . . Mr. Naofumi? What do you think of me?"

Huh? Ugh . . . Suddenly an image of Bitch flashed through my mind, and I was pissed off. It wasn't Raphtalia's fault though. Why did I have to think of that Bitch at a time like this? I didn't understand it myself.

"I feel like I work you too hard. That I push you too hard for a slave."

"Anything else?"

"I want to raise you to become a great person. You know, I want to take over for your parents."

I answered, but my tone of voice made it clear that I was a little confused by all the questioning. Raphtalia was making a weird face too.

"You said that you believed in me so . . . So I kind of think of you like my daughter. I want to take care of you."

We hadn't been together for all that long when you thought of it as a period of time. But I had known her since she was very small.

Like I've just mentioned, she looked like an adult now, but on the inside, she was still a kid. She was trying really hard to act like an adult, but without someone there to protect her, there were definitely things that she wouldn't be able to handle on her own.

"Oh, um . . . Okay! But wait, isn't that kind of weird?!"

"It's not weird. We have a long day tomorrow. Get some sleep."

"Okay."

She nodded and smiled, but I could tell she was still turning some doubt over in her mind. She slipped back into the carriage and tried to get some sleep.

I, for one, turned back to my compounding work.

Oh, that reminds me: as we'd been traveling around, we still were fighting monsters. We'd leveled up a bit lately.

Naofumi: Level 37
Raphtalia: Level 39
Filo: Level 38

Now even Filo was stronger than I was. Why did I level up so slowly?

No, it was just because the two of them were both attackers. And Filo was so quick and agile she could take enemies out in the blink of an eye. That was why she was leveling up so quickly. Raphtalia, too, rushed into combat—even to the point of ignoring my orders. Even still, she wasn't as fast as Filo.

"Master!"

"What is it, Filo?"

I was still working on my compounding when a sleepy Filo reverted to her human form and came to lean against me.

"Master! Aren't you sleepy yet?"

"I haven't finished compounding all this medicine yet. I'll sleep once I finish with this stuff."

"Oh . . ."

"You get some rest. You're working the most out of all of us, after all."

Even if she said that she liked pulling the carriage, that didn't change the fact that it was still hard physical labor. She said it was easy, but I still needed to think about her health.

"Aren't you lonely, being awake all by yourself?"

"It's all in how you think about it. I can watch you two sleep, and then I'm not so lonely myself."

"Really? Ahahaha."

Filo looked happy, and she giggled to herself. She didn't seem very excited though. Maybe I was just imagining it.

"What is it?"

"Master . . . .. Well, if you aren't lonely when you watch me sleep, then that's good!"

What the hell?

"Um . . . Master? What were you thinking about when you chose me?"

"What?"

I hadn't really been thinking of anything. I chose her at random.

Even further, I'd picked the egg thinking that I didn't care whether or not I got what I was looking for.

"You know what? I feel really lucky that I got picked by you."

Well, when you think about it, I felt pretty lucky too. She was a strong attacker. She was fun to have around, and cute too, and I felt myself growing parental to her too. I couldn't deny that.

Both Filo and Raphtalia were still just kids, even if they were on their way to looking like adults.

I knew that I really shouldn't have them fighting for me. It didn't matter what world we were in—regardless of the world, no one with a good heart would push little girls to the front lines of battle.

Did it even matter if they wanted it to be this way? I was in the wrong, and I knew it.

What I really should have done, had it been possible, was to make a safe place for Raphtalia where she could escape the horrors of battle.

But the reality was that I wasn't powerful enough to do that—and I didn't have enough money.

As for Filo—she was a normal girl now, and I didn't really have any business getting her to fight either. If we were free to do whatever we wanted, I'd just set her free. Monsters should get to do whatever they wanted to, like . . . pull carriages? I guess that wasn't so different from what we were actually doing.

Whatever . . . However you looked at it, I was the bad guy.

"Hey, you know what I heard? I heard that I was cheap."

"Huh?"

Filo just started talking.

The day I had left her at the slave trader's tent, she'd reached out her hands for where I'd been and was crying and calling for me. The slave trader had whispered to himself: "It's so strange . . . That egg I sold him was just some cheap thing . . . Why had it mutated so much?"

"Qweh?!"

The slave trader might not have known that Filo could understand human speech, so he had just blurted it out to an assistant of his.

"Let's double check this. This Filolial was from two flightless birds . . . and was supposed to be raised for her meat, correct?"

The assistant nodded.

"Well, the egg was worth 50 pieces of silver . . . same as an adult specimen . . ."

"Gwehhhhhh!"

Filo had flapped her wings in anger once she found out how little she was worth. She started balking.

"Is this all from the hero's power? Or is it because of the monster's meat she ate? She's turning all white too . . . Yes . . . if we are careful here, we could make a lot of money."

"What should we do with this Filolial?"

"We need to study her. Just think—a 50-pieces-of-silver specimen has advanced this much! What would happen if we supplied the Hero with a higher-quality sample? We could make even more money. The worst we could do is fix our weaker specimens and sell them for a higher price . . . but think what we could do if we gave him a better Filolial . . . or even better yet . . . a dragon!"

"Qwehhhhhhhhhhhhhhh?!"

"Oh no! The cage!"

Filo had gotten so upset that she broke her cage. I guess she wanted to show off how powerful she was . . . especially considering the way they were talking about her.

She wanted me to decide what she was worth. She'd do anything I asked. If I didn't, she didn't understand where she fit into the world. She wanted, more than anything, to emphasize that she was MY Filolial.

"Master . . . Don't abandon me. I want to stay with you . . ."

Her eyes were filled with tears. I tried to calm her down.

"If you behave yourself, I won't abandon you."

I had just chosen her at random, but you could also say that because of my actions she was now faced with a different fate than she would have had.

I wondered if she could have been bought by a normal customer and just lived her days out on a farm somewhere. Granted, if she was raised for her meat, it wouldn't have been an ideal life, but maybe that's just what life was like for Filolials.

When you think about it that way, it was all my fault. It was my fault that she had to throw herself into battle like this.

Was that . . . happiness? Being chosen for some role without your input is a tough hand to be dealt. I knew that first-hand. Who had asked me to be the Shield Hero?

"You promise? If I break my leg or something, you won't sell me off and buy yourself a new girl?"

"Yeah, I promise. And I don't lie . . . normally. Yeah, you're good."

"Yes! I'll do my best."

"I hope so."

And then she leaned against my back and started snoring.

C'mon . . . What was she so afraid of?

I suppose the real root of the problem was me. Sticking with Raphtalia and me, she must have been growing used to being told how awful we are and never getting a word of thanks.

Maybe she was afraid that I would think she was worthless, like the rest of the country seemed to consider us. Maybe she'd been afraid of that from the beginning.

But I was the one who was really afraid. What if Raphtalia and Filo just decided they didn't want to fight anymore?

I was contradicting myself. The only reason that I was able to fight was because Raphtalia and Filo were there with me. Maybe, originally, they didn't have to fight at all. But when I chose them from the slave trader's place, I changed their fates.

That was why I needed to think about my responsibility to them.

Once the world was at peace, I'd have to make a place for

them, a place where they could live out their days happily.

We arrived in the eastern territory.

The trees were all wilted and cracking, and the air felt heavy. It wasn't supposed to be particularly cold there, but the sky was black, and the whole land seemed bathed in darkness.

I looked to the sky, which was covered in a thick layer of clouds. We were approaching a mountain range. It felt ominous.

"Um . . ."

We reached a fork in the road and stopped to check the map.

"Filo, head toward the mountains."

"Okay!"

"Both of you get some cloth to cover your mouths—just in case. There's supposed to be a disease spreading around here."

"Okay."

I covered my own mouth with a strip of cloth as well and readied my nerves for defense, in case we needed that. We made for the farming village.

To simply describe the village, it was dark, the sky was covered in thick clouds, and the whole village was black and dark.

"Are you a merchant? I hate to . . . tell you this, but . . . our village is very sick. You should escape . . . cough . . . while you can."

A miserable-looking villager told us about the situation in between coughs.

"I know about all that. We've come to sell you medicine."

"Have you? Wonderful!"

The villager took off running, telling everyone that a medicine man had arrived.

Honestly, the place was looking pretty bad. I wasn't sure if we would have enough medicine to take care of everyone.

As if to further stimulate my insecurity, a wave of village voices swelled, calling for medicine.

"The bird-god carriage! We're saved!"

Oh no . . . With all these expectations, what if my medicine didn't work? They'd lose all trust in me.

Oh well.

"Who needs medicine?"

I climbed down from the carriage, explaining that my medicine was most effective when administered by myself.

"Over here, Beloved Saint."

Man, they were calling me a saint right from the get-go . . . Something about it made me uncomfortable. Even still, it was better than being the despised Shield Hero.

They led me to a long building filled with sick people. The building itself stood apart from the other buildings in the village.

A cemetery stood behind the building, and there were a number of fresh graves there.

If I said that it smelled like death, you would know what

I meant: that horrible atmosphere that hangs around hospitals and graveyards. I was confident that it was all the same.

I wasn't sure if my medicine would solve the problem here.

They were only intermediate recipes, so I shouldn't be overconfident with them. If the medicine didn't work, there was no backup plan. Or no . . . It would be expensive, but I could administer more expensive medicines to them.

I wished I could be more flexible with my products. I wish that I could make stronger medicines, even if it meant struggling through another book. It was better than running out of options. The next time I passed that apothecary, I'd have to ask if he would sell me a book of higher-level recipes.

"Please, help my wife!"

"Sure."

There was a woman there, coughing endlessly. I pulled her into a seating position and gave her some medicine.

Poof . . . A glowing light appeared, radiating out from her center.

Color returned to her face. Excellent. It must have worked.

"Next!"

I raised my eyes to see the villager standing there, a look of astonishment on his face.

"What is it?"

"I . . . um . . ."

The man pointed to a child lying down next to the woman.

The child had been coughing, just like the woman, but now the coughing had suddenly stopped.

Why? Did he die?

I leaned closer to check to see if the child was breathing. He was. Good, he was still alive.

But the child had been coughing so violently only a moment earlier. Now he appeared very calm.

"What happened?"

"When you, Beloved Saint, healed my wife, at the very same time, my child's coughing stopped."

Hm . . . could that have been because of the medicine efficacy range expansions (small) ability?

Expanding the range of a medicine . . . now that was an awesome ability.

It seemed like the medicine would be effective on anybody within a radius of one meter.

This shield had access to all sorts of tricky specs hidden away, didn't it?

But I bet that the ability wouldn't help very much in a battle because how often were we within a meter of one another in battle? The enemy would have to be pretty weak.

"Well that makes things easy! Anyone that needs healing, crowd around! This medicine will work on anyone within this circle here. We can cure everyone at once. Hurry up!"

"Yes sir!"

There weren't enough people there to help, so Raphtalia and Filo helped carry the sick to the center of the room, where I administered medicine to someone in the center.

It helped us save medicine, and it was easy and fast. With that one bottle, we'd managed to heal the entire building's worth of patients.

After some time had gone by, we realized that while everyone's symptoms had improved, no one had completely recovered from the disease. I wasn't sure what to do about that.

"I suppose that's about all I can do with the medicine I've got."

"Thank you so much!"

It was nice to have some gratitude, but I honestly wasn't totally satisfied with my results.

There was still a risk of infection, and we hadn't managed to eradicate the disease.

"Can you tell me where this disease came from? Is it endemic? Or is it contagious, and you caught it from a traveler?"

If the medicines I had weren't able to cure it, then it must have been a pretty severe disease. Who knows when we would catch it ourselves? In the worst case, we'd have to turn tail and get the hell out of there.

"Well, a doctor told us that the disease blew down on the wind from those mountains over there. Those mountains are full of monsters though."

"Tell me more."

"You can ask him yourself."

In my world, a doctor would have understood science and how to use it to cure people. Here, a doctor used magic to the same effect.

He had been working in the village for a while, trying to compound a medicine that would be effective on this new disease. Just as we'd arrived, he was holed up in that building with the patients, and he helped us out.

"Hey, can you make better medicine than an apothecary?"

"Yes, I'm making some right now. And yet, after seeing what you, Saint, were able to do with your own medicines, and the dramatic improvement among the villagers, I don't think my own project is necessary anymore."

"I'd get back to that as soon as you can. We haven't managed to completely cure the disease, which means it will probably come back."

"Yes sir!"

"Wait."

The doctor had run back to his tools and was about to enthusiastically throw himself back into his work when I called for him to wait.

"You said that this disease came down on the wind from the mountains. Why do you think so?"

"Yes, well . . . about a month ago the Sword Hero was in

these lands, and he slew a powerful dragon that had his territory in those mountains."

Oh yeah . . . I think I had heard something about that.

"Dragons typically make their nests far from human villages but this was a strange dragon."

"What does that have to do with anything?"

"Well, at the time, a great number of adventurers gathered here to watch the Sword Hero work. They climbed the mountain afterward, and everyone took pieces of the dragon with them."

I guess you could make really good weapons and equipment from dragon materials . . .

I was a little jealous, actually.

"And?"

"This is where it gets good. Everything was fine until the adventurers stripped the dragon down to its bones. It actually brought quite a lot of money to this poor village. The problem started when the dragon's remains started to rot. Some adventurers went to see the body, and they came back sick."

"So the dragon's body is the source of all this sickness?"

"I believe so."

If they had gone up there to strip off what would be good for equipment, then I can imagine what was left. The meat. No matter how awesome a dragon was, a dead dragon's meat would rot just like anything else.

There might have been connoisseurs out there that would

have a little interest in the meat, but the majority of it would be left to rot. I'd read in stories that dragon meat was so delicious that nothing would go to waste. But by the standards of this world, who knew? Maybe it was poisonous or something.

Then there would be the organs. Livers rot very quickly.

Ren would have been after more useful materials, so I am sure they left the organs there.

What about the heart? I felt like the heart was sure to have some sort of magical purpose.

"If you know what the problem is, why don't you take care of it?"

"The mountains are crawling with powerful monsters. You'd have to be a pretty experienced adventurer to go in there and hope to come out. None of these farmers are able to undertake such a task."

"Then why not get an adventurer to help you?"

"By the time we noticed, the whole ecology of the mountain range was thrown off balance. The air turned to poison, and the sickness is so strong, normal adventurers would never make it out. Not that they come anyway. Everyone is afraid of the disease, and no one comes by anymore."

Dammit, Ren . . . I sure wished he would clean up his own mess.

Ren was the youngest of us heroes. Had I been a high schooler, I probably wouldn't have given any thought to the lingering effects of dead dragon either. These effects wouldn't happen in the games he was used to, so I suppose it was to be expected.

"What should we do, Beloved Saint?"

"Did you send a report to the Crown?"

"Yes, we are waiting on a medicine delivery."

"What about the . . . heroes?"

"They are very busy, so we are probably not a high priority for them."

Whether it be Motoyasu or Itsuki or Ren . . . it didn't matter. They all pissed me off.

"Have you already sent money to the Crown for their support?"

"Yes . . ."

"If you cancel, will the money be returned?"

The doctor caught my eye and looked at me straight and deep.

"Are you going to take care of it, Beloved Saint?"

"Well, if it is going to be a while before the medicine arrives, I might as well. If I succeed, I'll accept your payment."

"All right . . . Well, it should take another half-day, at least."

"Okay great. I'm going to go take care of the dragon remains. I will take the money that you previously sent to the Crown."

"Yes sir."

And so we left for the mountains to see what we could do about the dragon remains.

Chapter Nineteen: Curse Series

"Wow! There are so many monsters!"

The surrounding lands had always been pretty barren, but once we were in the mountains everything was crumbling boulders.

There was a mountain path that led to the eastern countries, and because of it we were able to make progress, however slow.

We had been climbing through the mountains for thirty minutes or so.

I had brought restorative medicine, as well as healing medicine . . . and because the air was poisonous, I also brought some antidote.

Back in the village, before we left, I had declared my intention to leave the carriage behind.

"No! These carts are all filled with my most treasured memories!"

And Filo threw a fit until we agreed to let her pull the carriage.

How long had she even been alive? A month? And here she was telling me about life.

But I guess she had been pulling that carriage for more than 90% of the life she had lived, so it was only natural that she would have grown attached.

As for the monsters, there were a lot of poison trees and poison frogs . . . basically a lot of poisonous things.

After defeating them, I let the shield absorb what it could.

Poison Tree Shield: conditions met
Poison Frog Shield: conditions met
Poison Bee Shield: conditions met
Poison Fly Shield: conditions met

All the shields were poison-types, and the status booster abilities they came with related to Poison Resistance.

The only shield that broke the pattern was what I got from butchering the poison bee and letting the shield absorb the parts.

Bee Needle Shield II: conditions not met
Equip Bonus: attack 1
Special Effect: Needle Shield (small), Bee Poison (poison)

The defense rating hadn't changed much from the original Bee Needle Shield, but its special effect had changed from paralysis to poison.

But let's put all this aside for a moment. There were tons of monsters around. We'd beat them down, and more would come. Then we would beat THEM down and even MORE would appear.

The wind was full of disease, and it blew over the harsh landscape, which seemed to ooze poison from every crack and crevice. It would have been a difficult undertaking for an average adventurer.

"No matter how many we kill, there are more. Filo! Get us out of here!"

"Okay!"

Filo leaned into it and pulled at the carriage with all of her strength.

Running at full speed, an enemy or two got trampled here or there in the process. So we were actually still gaining a little experience.

Down the road we came upon a new monster that seemed to be made of mud, but Filo kicked it to the ground so quickly that I never got a chance to let the shield absorb it.

"We made it."

We'd found the dragon's corpse, and the air reeked of rot and poison and death.

The dragon was around ten meters and looked like what you picture when you think of a European dragon. Or it must have looked like that before it had died. It was hard to make it out in its current state.

It wasn't even possible to tell what color it had been, as the rot and decay were so far advanced. Here and there, blacked skin stuck to the bones.

It appeared to have been killed by a single strike to its belly. There was a deep cut there with rotting organs spilling from the open wound. It smelled horrible. There were clouds of Poison Flies gathered over the rotting meat, and the whole place looked really creepy.

"I'm hungryyyyy!"

"How can you look at this and say you're hungry?!"

Filo stuck her head into the carriage and started fishing around for something to munch on. I looked in after her.

"Raphtalia, you okay?"

"Yes."

Raphtalia had always had weak lungs, so I was worried that the air quality would bother her. But she said that she was feeling fine.

"If you don't feel good, make sure you lie down."

"Yes."

We beat back the Poison Flies and inched closer to the dragon corpse.

Ren and the other adventurers had already picked it over for materials. The horns and claws, scales, skin, and wings were pretty much gone. Even the tongue was gone. There was really only a pile of meat and bones left.

The skin was gone too, as if they'd taken it in one giant sheet.

The air smelled so bad we all twisted our noses up involuntarily. It was really awful.

I had abilities that lent me some Poison Resistance, but I wondered if Raphtalia would be all right.

"Filo, you take care of these flies while Raphtalia and I butcher what is left of the dragon. It's too big to use right now."

Had we buried it, it might continue to impact the land, and its rot could stay on the wind or in the water. No—better to absorb it into the shield and get rid of it.

"Okay."

Filo finished her carriage feast and nodded over her large, round belly.

"I feel kinda yucky."

"You ate too much."

Raphtalia and I moved closer to the corpse to set our plan into motion.

Rumble . . .

"Did I imagine that?"

"Um . . ."

I could have sworn that the corpse had . . . twitched?

It was probably an illusion caused by the shifting clouds of Poison Flies.

Rumble . . .

Nope. That was no illusion.

The dragon began to move and quickly settled itself into a defensive posture.

"Gaoooooooooooooh!"

The dragon had no claws or fangs, but it reared up and let out a ferocious roar.

"Why is this thing moving?!"

"Mr. Naofumi, you have to calm down!"

When the moving dead dragon, the Zombie Dragon, reared up in front of me, I discovered that I was screaming.

C'mon now. Give me a break. No matter how you looked at it, this dragon was too strong for us to take down as we were!

Zombie Dragons . . . I'd seen them in games before . . . and they were always stronger than the dragon had been before it died!

Would it be the same in this world?

The dragon rose to its feet, creaky and shaky, as all of its organs began to regenerate and resume their functions. Then it turned its face to us.

Now it had wings, and its tail was thrashing. Its claws and fangs would apparently take more time.

The rotting meat turned into liquid and flowed over the body, only to reform itself into wings and a tail. The same process was happening to its internal organs. I looked, and the fatal wound on its belly had already closed. How were we supposed to fight this thing?

"We're running!"

"But Filo has . . .!"

Raphtalia was frantically thrusting her finger in the direction of the Zombie Dragon.

I'd forgotten! Filolials and dragons never got along!

"Hiyaaa!"

Raphtalia had dashed for the dragon and run up its neck to deliver a solid kick to the head.

There was a loud and satisfying bash, and then the dragon began to bend over backward.

"Can we . . . win?"

Filo was a strong attacker, and this Zombie Dragon didn't have any claws or fangs yet.

Maybe we could win. I found it hard to believe that this dead dragon could hold out for very long.

And if we were to run from the beast now, there was a chance it might go on to attack the village.

Just like when Ren beat the dragon, the dragon would revive and make this place his territory again. But he was still regenerating, so this was our chance. If we didn't beat it now, the next adventurers wouldn't stand a chance.

"Don't be a fool! Back down!"

"I don't wanna!"

"Dammit! All right, let's take care of it!"

"Okay!"

Things were fine for a moment. I switched to the Chimera Viper Shield for its defense, and with that and my defense rating, I was able to stave off the dragon's attacks.

But then . . .

"Gaoooooooooooooh!"

Something in the belly swelled and moved up the throat. Then the beast opened its mouth and breathed a heavy purple gas in our direction.

Raphtalia and Filo did as we had agreed and rushed to hide behind my shield.

I held up the shield to block off the billowing gas, but . . .

"Wh . . . What is this?!"

"Cough! Cough!"

The breath was a thick and noxious poison.

I had Poison Resistance, and even I found my head reeling and my breath coming in ragged gasps.

Raphtalia began coughing violently behind me.

Filo was undeterred by the gas, or maybe she had been holding her breath. Regardless, she rushed forward and kicked hard at the dragon's soft underside.

"R . . . Raphtalia! Are you okay?"

"Cough, cough, cough!"

She was trying, through her tears, to say that she was all right. But she was unable to say anything. The coughing was too intense.

This wasn't good.

Filo and I could fight, but Raphtalia was incapacitated.

"Raphtalia, get out of here. Head back to the carriage—there's antidote in there. Take it and rest."

"Cough!"

Raphtalia fell into another coughing fit, but she desperately pointed at the dragon through the ragged coughs.

I followed her gaze and was dumbfounded.

The dragon had opened its wings and risen into the air, only to swoop down and scoop Filo up into its mouth.

The whole scene seemed to move in slow motion.

I threw out my hand, but . . .

"Ah . . ."

Crunch!

There was a deafening sound, and a wave of red liquid streamed from the dragon's mouth.

"Filooooooooo!"

It was either Raphtalia or me that screamed. I don't remember. Everything was a slow, confusing blur, and I couldn't be sure who was doing what.

That selfish, childish little bird had only been alive for a month, but she'd wanted to be with me the whole time. She wanted me to spoil her. She didn't want me to think her useless. She was just a little kid.

Like a revolving light show, my memories of Filo came flashing back to me.

What had happened?

What had . . .

The dragon chewed heavily on its catch, and then . . .

Gulp.

With a loud sound, it swallowed.

"No! Filo!"

My voice came wheezing from my mouth, and I stood still—shocked. It hurt. It hurt like I'd been kicked off a cliff. I feel like I finally understood what it meant to feel devastated, to feel hopeless.

It wasn't devastation that spurs you to action or to revenge. It was deeper and sadder. It was the devastation that the clock couldn't be turned back.

"Mr. Naofumi!"

Raphtalia turned to me and slapped me hard across the face.

"Get a hold of yourself! This isn't the time to be distracted!"

Her eyes were filled with tears.

She was yelling at me. She was saying that things would only get worse if we didn't do something.

But I couldn't hear her. I was overcome with anger . . . anger at losing my close friend right before my eyes.

You want power?

I could hear a voice speaking to me from my shield.

My eyes wandered down to look at the shield. I could hear the voice again.

Do you hate everything?

I felt my heart pound.

I could feel darkness expanding from the depths of the shield.

This had happened before, back when I had dueled with Motoyasu.

The shield's tree suddenly appeared before my eyes.

The screen turned around, and the reverse was some color, almost red, almost black—with another tree on it.

Curse Series.

The phrase ran through my mind quickly. There was one shield listed on the tree that was shining.

<u>Curse Series</u>
Shield of Rage: ability locked: equip bonus: skill "Change Shield (attack)," "Iron Maiden"
Special Effect: Self Curse, Burning Strength Up
Born from the heart: Shield of Murder . . .

This shield came with its own description and instruction. I didn't know if I had willed it or if it had been involuntary. But I followed my heart and discovered that the shield was already in my hand.

The Shield of Rage.

A great outpouring of emotion came from the shield, and the shield emitted a strong red-black light as it changed form.

The shield was covered in ominous-looking flames, and it was blood-red.

Thump . . . Thump . . .

My whole being was covered in anger, steeped in anger . . .

The last time, when I lost to Motoyasu and they were threatening to take Raphtalia away from me . . . when I had only hatred for everything in the world . . .

Everything in the world had looked black and seemed to be made of shadows . . . shadows that mocked me and hated me.

I was overcome with that emotion.

"Gaoooooooooooooh!"

An enormous black shadow turned to me and howled. It was reaching for me . . ..

"Haooooooooooooooooooooooooooooooooh!"

Chapter Twenty: The Shield of Rage

As if to match the howling of the beast, I let out a scream and accepted its attack with my shield.

It didn't hurt at all.

"Gaah?!"

The black shadow had been laughing at me, mocking me, but now it contorted its mouth in confusion and shock.

Hilarious.

"Die!"

I caught him by the arm and flung him away with all the strength I could muster.

The huge shadow let out a shriek of surprise as it flew through the air.

"Gaoooooh!"

But instead of realizing that it should think before attacking me again, it rose to its feet and came running at me.

I wondered . . . Could I still not attack anyone? Even with this shield?

I couldn't.

The beast turned and made to knock me over with a sweep of its tail.

"That won't work!"

The tail bounced off with an ineffectual clang. Its attacks wouldn't work on me.

"Useless!"

I had no way to beat the monster.

Or so I had thought. Suddenly a large whirlwind of black fire spiraled skyward with me at its center. It set the shadow's tail and arms ablaze.

"GAOOH?!"

The shadow fell to the ground in surprise.

"Heh . . . If the attack is this strong, I wonder if it can counter-attack."

The shadow was backing away from me, suddenly intimidated.

"Ha! Now you beg for your life?! You'll get no forgiveness from me!"

I shouted the title of my new skill.

"Iron Maiden!"

But the skill did not activate. Rather, the skill tree appeared before my eyes.

Shield Prison: Change Shield (attack): Iron Maiden

What was this? There were conditions on its use?

What a pain. If that was how it was, I'd just let the shadow attack me and try to get a counter-attack to activate.

"Just you wait . . . I'll kill you for sure!"

As I approached, the shadow behaved as though it was afraid of my anger, my murderous intention. It flung its arms about wildly.

Its arm connected with the shield and suddenly burst into flames.

The meat burned up, and the bones melted.

The flames weren't strong enough. I wanted to completely eradicate the beast.

"!"

I got it! The Shield of Rage was stronger the more enraged I was. The attack would rise, and the crazier I felt.

Well, that was easy for me.

All I needed to do was think about how THEY made me feel.

Myne Sufia . . . I guess her real name was Malty.

Just thinking of her name filled me with rage.

Next was Trash . . . Then Motoyasu, Ren, Itsuki . . .

I went over all that they had done to me, one memory at a time . . .

I hated them . . . I wanted to kill them . . .

The blood-red shield was reacting to my hatred and turning black.

"This time I'll really kill them . . . All of them . . ."

I caught the shadow by the arm and turned all my hatred into glowing coals.

The coals flew out from the shield and completely covered the shadow, swallowing it whole.

Then I felt something, right there on my hand, something warm. My black hatred started to melt away.

Thump . . .

It was . . . kind . . .

"Even if the whole world turns against you, I won't. I'll say it time and again: Mr. Naofumi didn't do it."

What?

At the sound of the voice, the darkened, warped world before me began to waver.

Somewhere in my heart, I knew that giving myself over to anger would result in losing something even more important.

I wanted to ignore it . . . and yet . . .

"Please, believe me. I have confidence in Mr. Naofumi. He hasn't committed any crime. He gave me medicine and saved my life. He taught me how to fight, how to survive. He is the great Shield Hero. I am your sword. No matter how hard the path, I'll walk it with you."

The voice was whispering to me.

I can't allow myself to be swallowed by hatred. I still had things I needed to protect.

Your anger weakens . . .

I can't forget it. But . . . But I want to give myself over to those who believe in me.

Would you refuse me?

I don't like orders. I'll choose my own path!

I'm always watching. Watching for your weakness.

The dark voice vanished, and some light returned to the world.

"Cough! Cough!"

I came back to my senses. Raphtalia was next to me, coughing violently and holding my hand in hers.

"Are you all right?"

"Yes . . . Yes, I'm . . .. fine. Cough!"

She'd been burned badly. But there were no enemies here that used fire.

What could it . . . No!

The special effect of the Shield of Rage, Self Curse . . . It must have hurt her too!

"Raphtalia! Why were you holding on to my hand?!"

"I thought that you . . . That you would disappear if I . . . If I didn't . . . Cough!"

Raphtalia smiled, then collapsed to the ground.

It was my fault . . . My fault that Raphtalia was hurt!

"I am the source of all power. Hear my words and understand them. Heal her!"

"First Heal!"

"I am the source of all power. Hear my words and understand them. Heal her!"

"First Heal!"

"I am the source of all power. Hear my words and understand them. Heal her!"

"First Heal!"

"I am the source of all power. Hear my words and understand them. Heal her!"

"First Heal!"

I kept casting the spell until I ran out of magic power.

Raphtalia . . . Raphtalia was the only person who believed in me. She was important to me!

The burns were bad. My low-level magic wasn't enough to heal them. I ran to the carriage to get the healing ointment.

"Gaoooooooh!"

I spun to see the dragon there, howling and swinging his burned arm at me and preparing to unleash its poison breath.

"Out of my way!"

I threw my arm up to catch the Zombie Dragon's attack. When I did, the shield began to shine with a black light and nearly activated the Self Curse Burning skill.

"Stop!"

The shield fell silent at my shout.

Had the flames erupted then and there, they would have killed Raphtalia. That wouldn't be good at all. But with how weak Raphtalia was, I didn't know if she could survive a blast from its poison breath.

As if the shield knew what I was thinking, it activated the Self Curse Burning, but only burned the streaming cloud of poison gas. It wasn't strong enough to actually kill the dragon though.

What to do?

The shield was constantly absorbing my hatred and anger, inflaming them. I was able to keep from being completely swallowed by them only with an enormous effort. How long before I was consumed by it?

But right now, I had to get to the carriage and get medicine for Raphtalia.

My need to protect Raphtalia was just barely strong enough to keep the anger at bay.

"Gah?!"

We were trading blows and then, in the middle of the fight, the dragon let out a terrible voice of confusion and pain.

"Wh . . . What the . . ."

What was happening? Did this mean that the Self Curse Burning was consuming the dragon?

"Gaoooooooooooh!!!"

Finally, the Zombie Dragon stopped moving altogether and returned to its skeletal form.

But this was no time to stand back and reflect on the battle.

The clouds of Poison Flies were nowhere to be seen. The raging dragon must have scared them off.

I held Raphtalia against me, ran for the carriage, found the healing ointment, and quickly applied it to her burns. Then I gave her the antidote.

"Oh . . . Mr. Naofumi . . ."

Her breathing had grown more regular, and she opened her eyes and smiled.

"Are you all right?!"

"Yes . . . Thanks to your medicine . . ."

And yet her wounds still looked pretty bad. The wounds themselves seemed to have shrunk and healed over from the medicine, but there were black scars remaining, maybe because of the black magic the shield had used. Anyway, the burns still didn't look very good.

"Don't . . . worry about me . . . Take care of the dragon."

"The dragon isn't moving anymore."

"Oh . . . then . . . then hurry and get rid of the skeleton."

"Okay."

Her eyes were insistent, desperate. They drove the point home: I had to do something.

"Are you okay staying here for now?"

"I can protect myself if I need to."

"Good . . . Good."

I climbed down from the carriage and walked in the direction of the dragon corpse.

I needed to butcher it and get the shield to absorb it all.

And Filo . . . At the very least, I wanted to recover her body and give her a proper burial.

I approached the corpse and could see that the internal organs were still twitching and squirming.

What was going on? There might be a way for me to fight it.

The Shield of Rage.

This dangerous shield that threatened to consume my heart also happened to have a fantastic defense rating and a strong counter-attack.

My heart couldn't take it, so I had switched my shield back to the Chimera Viper Shield. But I was ready to switch back at any time . . . if I needed to.

The wriggling internals moved, then stopped. Then they shook with such force I thought the stomach would tear . . . Then . . . Then I could see . . .

"Huff!"

It was . . . a bird that I knew on its side. She was covered in the rotted liquid of the dead dragon.

"Huff! I finally made it out!"

Filo seemed to be in a good mood and just fine, despite climbing from the stomach of the beast that had eaten her.

"Filo?! Are you all right? Are you hurt?!"

"I'm fine!"

"Then . . . Then what was all that blood when the dragon ate you?"

"Blood? Oh, yeah, when the dragon swallowed me it pushed on my tummy and I threw up."

What had she been eating? Oh yeah, all those tomatoes! That must have looked like blood.

That's right . . . She'd been stuffing her face with them for hours.

"Don't scare me like that! I thought you were dead!"

"An attack like that? That didn't hurt one bit!"

This bird was a monster. I guess she really was a monster.

Man . . . She'd really given me a scare.

"Master, were you worried about me?"

"Whatever."

"Master! You're embarrassed!"

"Want me to give the eulogy at your funeral?"

"No! But I'm happy! Don't you start thinking about buying a replacement for me!"

Right . . . Well, she was okay.

Filo stood there smiling, which annoyed me. She better remember all this.

"Anyway, what happened?"

"Well, the dragon swallowed me, and then, when I was in his tummy, I walked around and found this weird, glowing purple crystal."

Could it be that the dead dragon was reanimated by this purple crystal?

Filo had ripped her way out of the corpse. In its chest . . . Could it have been the heart?

But why?

Because it was a dragon? Even though it was dead, could it be that the dragon's latent magical power had gathered in the heart and crystallized?

"So what was with the crystal?"

"Ugh! Blech!"

I guess that was the answer . . . She'd eaten it. Her stomach looked like it was glowing too.

Geez . . . I could have hit her.

"There was a little left over. Does Master want a snack?"

She held out her little wing, and there was a purple crystal shard there in her hand.

What the hell?

I broke it in half and let the shield absorb it.

I knew it . . . My tree wasn't advanced enough to unlock anything.

"Raphtalia is hurt, so you and I are going to clean up this dragon."

"Okay!"

I swear . . . This bird was going to put me in the madhouse.

Good thing I didn't let myself get consumed by anger.

I'd switched to the Curse Shield to avenge Filo, but I'd almost been completely consumed by hatred.

If Raphtalia hadn't stopped me, I would have burned the dragon completely . . . and burned Filo too.

Rage . . . That shield was cursed.

It took me over to accomplish its own ends.

Had I let it take me over, I would have gone on to kill the other heroes when I finished with the dragon.

"Yummy!"

"Filo! That meat is rotten. Don't eat it!"

"Meat that's just starting to rot is the best kind, Master!"

"It's not 'just starting.' It's completely rotten!"

We kept on cleaning in our half-hearted, playful way. Soon enough, the dragon was gone.

I'd absorbed everything I could, but the tree wasn't advanced enough to unlock anything.

Even still, the bones and skin seemed like they would be useful materials, so I took a portion of them and loaded up the carriage.

Epilogue: As a Shield . . .

"Yes, it's a curse."

We returned to the village and rushed to the doctor to see if we could get treatment for Raphtalia.

"It's also very strong. The mountain dragon was in possession of such a powerful curse?"

"Well . . . No . . . Actually . . ."

I wasn't sure if I should be honest about what happened. I was at a loss.

"Yes, I accidentally let the dragon's meat touch me, and it burned me like this . . ."

Raphtalia spoke out and caught my eye as if to confirm that it would be our secret.

"Can you do anything for her? We can pay whatever you need."

Raphtalia was a girl. She didn't deserve to go through life covered with these dark, horrible scars.

"Well, there is one thing . . ."

The doctor went back into his room and returned with a bottle that was filled with a clear liquid.

"This is very strong . . . I don't know if it will heal her though."

"What is it?"

"Holy water. Curses are best removed by holy power . . ."

"Oh . . ."

The Shield of Rage would not only hurt its victims; it would curse their wounds so that they wouldn't heal.

It was sounding more and more dangerous. It was imbued with a counter-attack that didn't distinguish between enemy and ally.

And I'd seen the shield's tree, and it had not progressed at all.

It had only been for a short time, but now I knew that I couldn't unlock that shield.

"We'll soak these bandages in holy water for now . . ."

He did so, then took the sopping bandages and wrapped them around Raphtalia's dark scars.

"I can't say for sure if this will work . . . If you are able to, you should go to a large city and procure yourself some holy water made by the church."

"How much would we need to heal her?"

"Honestly . . . the curse is very strong. I don't know if you can cure it . . . How did the dragon . . .?"

It had been me . . . It was my fault. But apparently the curse was strong enough that people would believe that it was done by a dragon.

"Okay . . . How much medicine have you made?"

"I've just made a little. Beloved Saint, please help the sick."

"Sure."

I left Raphtalia with the doctor and went to the building that was filled with sick people.

You could tell that the medicine had been made by a professional.

It completely healed the disease that I had been unable to take care of with my own medicine.

I watched the patients there, sleeping soundly, and felt relieved.

I wanted strength . . . I wanted to be strong enough that I wouldn't have to depend on that shield.

I wanted to be able to heal people, not curse them! It was because of my weakness. That was the root of it. I hated my weakness.

Filo had survived. She was fine. But there would be a time when she wasn't, when she would need me. When she vanished from before my eyes, I completely lost myself.

I let the thought linger in my mind. This was no game.

If someone dies, they won't come back to life. I found myself staring at the cemetery behind the building.

They'd betrayed me . . . tricked me! That was even more reason for me to . . . to protect the people who believed in me.

I went back to the doctor's and found Raphtalia sitting there, wrapped in bandages. I apologized.

"I'm sorry."

"It's okay."

"But I . . ."

"I was more afraid of you leaving . . . of you going some-where far away from me."

"What?"

"That power . . . It wants to take you somewhere far away. That's what I felt, anyway. So if I was able to stop you, to keep you here, then these scrapes are a fair price to pay."

She smiled, and I felt a sharp pang of emotion.

I had to protect her. I HAD to. I made up my mind never to lose myself to that shield.

And then . . . I realized that running from loss . . . that run-ning from loss was a kind of loss itself.

"Raphtalia . . . You jumped into battle to prevent this, didn't you?"

"What?"

"When we fought the dragon, I ordered you to retreat. But if you had, you couldn't have protected me."

I'd been wrong. Just protecting . . . just running . . . wouldn't be enough.

All I could do was protect.

But . . . But as I protected them, I needed to make sure the enemies were defeated . . . so that I wouldn't lose my friends.

All this . . . all this pain was because I wanted to run from loss.

"You're wrong! I . . . I ran ahead for you to satisfy myself."

Raphtalia leaned forward and forcefully rejected my theory.

"Courage and recklessness are not the same thing. I've been reckless, and you kept trying to reign me in to protect me . . . But I . . . But I . . ."

Without even thinking about it, I reached out and touched her cheek. A tear raced over my fingers.

"Just like courage and recklessness are different, so are caution and cowardice. You're no coward. No one can protect a coward."

So I wanted to lead the charge. I wanted to stand at the front so that I might protect Filo and Raphtalia.

Back on the mountain, had I been at the front, I could have sent out an Air Strike Shield, and Filo could have used it as a springboard. Then the dragon wouldn't have eaten her.

I was afraid of losing her.

"So don't worry about it. Look at how much practice we got, and we didn't lose anyone. We can use what we've learned in the future. We're stronger today than we were yesterday."

Raphtalia's eyes filled with tears, and she nodded along.

"Yes . . . Don't rush too far ahead . . . Don't hang too far back . . . It's a difficult balance."

"It is, but I think we can do it. Just remember that the Shield Hero, that's me, stands at the front of the line. Protect yourself, and if you find yourself free, protect others. That's easy."

"When you put it that way, it does sound easy."

"It will be easy."

"Is Big Sister okay?"

Filo had stuck her head into the room and was looking over at Raphtalia nervously.

"I'm okay."

This would be a day for Raphtalia to rest up. Filo and I went outside.

"Master!"

"What?"

"I used to think that I wished I could stay a human forever . . . because you and her are so close."

She was in human form and was smiling.

"But I couldn't. It's fun to pull the carriage, and I was just fooling myself because I wanted you to like me. Even if I pretend to be like you, I can't do it!"

" . . ."

"But, Master? I'm the same Filo, no matter what shape I am."

"That's true."

I'd been surprised when she'd turned into a human, but I don't think I had treated her any differently. Even still, I did treat her like a child.

"I'm me, Master is Master, and Big Sister is Big Sister, right? You can't be anyone but who you are, and I . . . I can't be a real person. But even still, there's no one out there that can replace me, is there?"

THAT'S why she'd turned into a person?

I nodded in response to her barrage of questions.

"But you know what? I like you, Master! I like you just as much as Big Sister does! I'm going to be the best Filo I can be!"

"That's . . . good."

Who would have thought Filo would lecture me on these things?

Protecting everyone was supposed to be MY job, but I noticed, with amazement, that I wasn't upset with having the job stolen from me. I wonder why.

"You know what? For Master and Big Sister, I'm going to do all I can! I'm gonna try real hard. Yup!"

"You better. Protecting you is my job, after all."

"Yup!"

We spent the rest of the day relaxing in the village.

The next day we worked hard to try and wipe out the disease for good.

The doctor asked me if I could do anything, and I set about making medicines. We ended up finishing earlier than we'd thought we could. I had thought that he could teach me something about medicine and healing, but I didn't know enough, and I didn't want to be in the way.

"Thank you so much, Beloved Saint!"

A young girl from the sick house waved to me and said thank you.

Did I . . . protect them?

I made up my mind not to run. If I ran, I couldn't protect the people I needed to protect, and I'd just save my own life—but make it not worth living.

I wasn't alone anymore.

I was a parent to Raphtalia and Filo now, and I needed to do whatever I could to make the world better for them, to make it into a place where people could live out their lives in happiness.

"Mr. Naofumi?"

"Master!"

"Huh? What's up?"

I'd been walking around the peaceful village when Raphtalia and Filo called out to me.

"You looked really . . . concerned?"

"Yeah!"

"Don't worry about it."

"But, Master! You're such a worrywart! Of course we worry."

"A worrywart?"

"Yeah. These days all you ever say to us is, 'Are you all right?'"

"She's right. But you don't need to worry anymore."

"But I . . ."

"Don't treat us like children anymore. We are thinking about our own affairs."

"Yeah!"

"I know now that you care about us . . . but in the exact same way, we care about you too, Mr. Naofumi. We'll be fine if we stick together."

"Yeah!"

"You're right."

Raphtalia was growing. She had her own thoughts and her own feelings, like her inner maturity had caught up to her appearance. I couldn't treat her like a child anymore.

We were a team now. I guess.

Worrying about things on my own wasn't going to do anyone any good. I couldn't bring peace to the world by myself. One look at the waves of destruction made that immediately apparent, and it was even more true for me, the Shield Hero, who couldn't even attack on his own.

If we wanted a world of peace, we'd have to make it together.

"All right. Let's do this . . . together."

"Oh! Master smiled!"

"She's right. And it wasn't some weird, fake smile, either. That was real."

The two of them were smiling back at me.

Heh . . . Was that supposed to be me? Did I never smile?

Whatever.

I was smiling now.

I wasn't alone anymore, because I had friends I could depend on.

Extra Chapter: Presents

"Mr. Naofumi, I can see steam."

That day we'd been rolling down the road in Filo's carriage when I spoke to Mr. Naofumi.

He'd said that we were on our way to a town with hot springs, and I was getting excited to arrive.

"Huh? Already?"

"It's stinky!"

Filo looked back from her place at the front of the carriage and made a face.

"That's sulfur. Hot springs often smell like that."

"Are hot springs yummy?"

"Hot springs aren't very yummy on their own. Hot spring eggs are good though."

"Hot springs lay eggs?"

"No, no. They boil the eggs in the hot springs. There are hot spring rice cakes too, though maybe not in this world."

Mr. Naofumi was taking his time and responding to each of Filo's questions.

"We're going to sell medicine here, right?"

"Yeah. I'm going to get us a room at the inn. Raphtalia, you take care of the sales."

"Okay."

"Considering that it's a hot spring and all, we should take a little break and relax here. Two or three days should do it."

Filo and I broke into giggles.

We'd been traveling so much lately we didn't really get any time to relax.

Especially Mr. Naofumi. He was always making medicines or working through the accounting books or studying magic. He didn't get to rest at all.

I thought that taking a few days to relax sounded like a great idea.

"That sounds like a wonderful idea, Mr. Naofumi."

"So we can play tomorrow, right, Master?"

"Well, I still need to work on these medicines, so I can't relax too much. But I can probably stand a good soak in the springs. Filo, get ready to stop."

"Okay!"

There were many doctors and caretakers visiting the springs, and they bought Mr. Naofumi's medicines from us quickly. Soon, we were sold out.

So we went back to the inn and went for a soak in the springs.

"I'm going to go see Master!"

"No, you can't. You'll just annoy him."

"But it will be fine. He likes me."

"What will be fine?! That's the men's bath. You're a girl, right?"

But Filo wasn't listening. She had climbed up on the fence dividing the baths and jumped over to the other side.

"Master! Let's play!"

"Filo? Oh, okay. Make sure you get way down in the water. You want to be up to your neck."

"Okay."

I could hear Mr. Naofumi's and Filo's voices coming from the other side of the partition.

What the . . . I sort of felt like I had lost.

I sat in the water and let my eyes wander to a sign in the corner. It detailed the history of the spring.

There had been a silver boar? When the villagers defeated the boar, the hot springs appeared where he'd fallen. The history was written like an old story.

It also said that the hot spring was a spring of love.

If a man and woman entered the spring together, they'd be bonded for life.

And now Filo and Mr. Naofumi were soaking in it together!

"Ugh . . ."

I was starting to feel hot from sitting in the water for too long, so I decided to get out.

When I got back to the room, Mr. Naofumi was there too, having left the baths early himself. He was studying accessory-making.

He's learned a whole bunch of stuff, but lately he hadn't made anything of quality because we didn't have any good material.

"Hey, Raphtalia. Come take a look at this."

He noticed me come into the room and indicated that I should sit next to him on the bed. He had a bottle of medicine in his hand.

"Okay."

Mr. Naofumi had noticed how bad the scars on my back were, and so he applied medicine to them.

Thanks to his effort, the skin on my back now felt much better than it had.

Suddenly the story of the couple in the hot springs came back to me.

"Mr. Naofumi . . ."

I gathered my courage and dropped the towel I was wrapped in. I wanted him to see me.

He had trauma from a past relationship with women, and so I wasn't sure how he would feel about this kind of thing.

But I wanted him to know how I felt, so I just followed my heart and acted.

"What . . . What do you think . . .?"

Aren't I . . . attractive? Mr. Naofumi . . .

Mr. Naofumi was watching my back, and he seemed at a loss. I was sure he knew what I meant, and I was waiting for his answer . . .

"Well, I think it's looking a lot better. You've changed so much since we first met."

So he . . . Mr. Naofumi looked at my nakedness without

even flinching. He just looked at me, observing.

Actually, I was the one getting emotional. I felt dizzy.

"Oh? Is that . . . um . . . all?"

"What else is there?"

"Oh, nothing."

"If you don't get dressed, then you'll catch a cold . . ."

"Ah! Big Sister is naked!"

Filo entered the room and threw a fit.

She jumped out of her dress to get naked herself, then ran straight at me. This wasn't a game!

"I want to play too!"

"No! Stop it!"

Oh no . . . I was so close to making my deep confession to Mr. Naofumi.

Evening fell, and we got ready for bed. Filo was already deep asleep next to me.

"Um . . . Mr. Naofumi?"

"What?"

He was still making medicines and wouldn't sleep for a while.

This was my chance. I had to let him know how I felt!

"Um . . ."

"Huh?"

Mr. Naofumi was looking at me.

Maybe it was because of the hot springs, but my face felt hot. I felt like I was boiling, but I had to try.

"Mr. Naofumi I . . . I . . . I like you."

"Oh yeah?"

I did it! He knew! I felt like my heart could fly.

"I like you too . . . Like a daughter."

It was like he'd thrown water on me. I sunk to the floor.

Ah . . . He treated me like a kid because he thought he was my parent.

But I'm not a child anymore! I'd told him that time and time again, and yet . . .

"Yeah, you're an adult now . . ."

Right, he'd never say that to me.

He was so . . . dumb! But that was what was so great about him.

I . . . I wanted to take another step, but it didn't seem like the time. I didn't think it would work.

The ideal would be him coming to me and telling me he loved me. But that would never happen because of the trauma he'd experienced. So I would have to tell him first—then we could be together.

But what would I have to do to get him to notice?

Then I remembered a story I'd heard when I was a little girl.

My mother had said that she had realized she was in love when my father got her a present.

Yes. That was when I decided what I should do.

I'd have to get him a present that would wake him up and make him notice me!

Mr. Naofumi let his shield absorb all kinds of things because it would make him stronger. So I'd have to find something that would make me stronger, more powerful, so that he'd realize I was an adult when I confessed! Then he would notice me!

The next day I walked around the town and tried to gather information.

"Are there any rare materials around?"

Had I just picked some normal or well-known item, Mr. Naofumi wouldn't be impressed. I needed something legendary.

When we set out to make Filo's clothes, we'd had to go exploring in ruins. If I found something similar . . . something that couldn't be procured without a bit of danger . . . Yes . . . then he would notice me!

"Something rare? Well the Gaggoko hot spring eggs are pretty famous and delicious."

The innkeeper thought for a moment before he answered me.

"That's not what I mean. I mean something more . . . rare. Like a pretty stone or something?"

"Maybe like Lachium?"

"What is that?"

"It's a very rare mineral that can only be found in these parts. Wizards and alchemists will pay very high prices for it. Locals value it because it's supposed to help people in their love lives."

That's it! If I found something so rare and valuable by myself, Mr. Naofumi was sure to be impressed!

And it helped with your love life? Perfect.

"Where can you find it?"

"I hear you can find it off in the mountains. But it's pretty difficult to find."

"I know."

"They say you can find Lachium in Gaggoko nests."

I kept on asking questions until I found out where you could find the Lachium ore.

Then I got ready and left to find it.

"Should be somewhere around here . . ."

I held a map in one hand while I climbed a volcano.

It smelled like sulfur and was hot.

The innkeeper had said that there was a monster that lived at very high elevations and that you would have a very good chance of finding Lachium under its nest.

That monster itself was not uncommon, but it was uncommon to make nests. It would be drawn to the spot by the magic in the stone.

Then I found it . . . the nest I was looking for.

"Ah . . ."

Because I was looking off at the nest, I'd turned my eyes high above me, and then, with a bang, I ran straight into something.

"Ouch."

I fell off my feet and hurt my butt. Then I looked up at the thing that I'd hit.

"Oh . . . Big Sister!"

Filo was standing there with a paper in her hand just like me.

The paper was probably a map.

"Filo?! What are you doing here?"

"That's what I was about to ask you!"

" . . ."

What was going on? My women's intuition started whispering in my ear.

It said that Filo was my enemy, that she was trying to take Mr. Naofumi away from me.

And she'd been saying it for weeks. She'd never let me have Mr. Naofumi.

I had to get to the bottom of this.

"Filo, I'll ask you again. What are you doing here?"

"I, um . . . I heard that there was a rare kind of food up here!"

Now that she mentioned it, the innkeeper had mentioned something about a Gaggako hot spring egg.

That must be what she was talking about.

"If I bring that delicious and rare food to Mr. Naofumi, he'll pat me on the head and tell me that I'm his favorite!"

"He will not!"

What was this kid thinking?

"What about you, Big Sister? What are you doing out here?! You're keeping secrets!"

Filo turned her head in confusion, and I had to admit that she was kind of cute. But if I lost Mr. Naofumi to this cute face, I'd be in misery.

Whatever happened, I just couldn't lose to her!

"Fine then. Let's see whose present Mr. Naofumi likes the best!"

"Fine! I won't lose."

The competition was on.

"Hiyaaaaaaaaaah!"

"I won't lose!"

Filo started running up the sharp incline, and I ran after her. I overtook her soon enough.

This is what I trained for, moments like this!

Even if Filo died, I wasn't going to lose to her.

"Guggaga?!"

The Gaggoko screamed when it saw us running for it. It was a large, round, white bird.

"Out of my way!"

"Excuse us!"

Filo ran into the nest, but I reached under it for the shining stone I saw there.

But just then a monster appeared behind us, drawn by our shouts and filled with murderous rage. It ran at us.

"What the . . ."

We both looked at each other, as if to confirm what we were seeing. We'd taken too long to notice.

"Buruheeeeeeeeeeeeee!"

It was a silver boar.

The Silver Razorback had been drawn by our shouts and was running straight for us.

It was bigger than Filo.

What would happen if a monster that large ran straight into a Gaggoko nest?

The whole nest, with us in it, flew into the air. We were suspended there, in the air, for a moment.

I had seen it. Under the Gaggoko nest, there had been a large, shining stone. It must have been the Lachium ore.

I saw that same ore now, shattered to dust by the impact, raining down around us.

At the same time, the egg that Filo had been looking for flew past us, suspended in the air like everything else.

"Gugguga! Gugguga!"

The Gaggoka raised its wings and flew away.

Then, with a crash, we all fell down to that steep slope . . .

"Ah . . .."

"Ugh! The eggs! Our food!"

We both realized that we'd lost the things we'd come for. We both looked to the source of our failure and then looked to one another.

"Big Sister . . ."

"Yeah . . ."

The Silver Razorback seemed to understand that he was in danger now, with all our wrath directed at him.

"Buruhee?"

The boar began to tentatively step backward.

Had he turned and fled slowly, he must have known that death was waiting for him.

But even if he did turn and flee—that wouldn't change his fate.

The Silver Razorback turned . . .

"Hey! He's running!"

"You think you're getting out of here alive?"

"Buruheeeeeeeeeeeeeeeeeeee!"

The boar let out a terrified scream.

"Whew, that was tough."

"Ugh . . . the egg!"

We looked all around the mountains after our encounter but never found what we were looking for.

At the very least, we had a local Silver Razorback to take back with us. I let Filo carry it.

"Where did you two go? I've been looking for you."

Mr. Naofumi was waiting for us at the gate to the town.

"Oh you know . . ."

"Huh? What's that, Filo? I've never seen a monster like that before. Let's butcher it and let the shield absorb it."

"Okay."

"Uh huh. Well, I was in the mountains looking for something when this thing showed up and gave us trouble. Me and Raphtalia took care of it."

"Wow! Or would you rather butcher it and eat it? It looks like a boar, so we could make boar stew."

"Yeah! That sounds good! Make it!"

"Ahhhhhhhhhhhhhhhh!"

There was a crowd of people pointing, shouting, and running at us.

"Dammit! Let's run!"

"Okay!"

Mr. Naofumi and I took off running.

The both of us did not have a very good reputation in Melromarc, so we ran into people that hated us pretty often.

So we were used to treatment that way, and when we saw people pointing at us, we ran off instinctively.

But . . .

"Please wait! Wait! Please, please stop!"

Something seemed strange. So we stopped.

Then we noticed that the villagers were smiling and beckoning for us to come back.

"You have hunted a Silver Lord for us!"

"Silver Lord?"

"Yes, it's a beast that we use in a prosperity ceremony in these parts. Will you let us have it?"

Yeah . . . When we'd been in the hot spring, I think I'd seen a picture detailing something like that.

So this was the monster from the picture.

The villagers insisted that the boar was not particularly good for materials but that they would buy it from us for a good price.

In the end, Mr. Naofumi and all the villagers praised me and Filo for our job. Mr. Naofumi sold the boar to them and even gave us all the money from it.

"Um . . ."

"We were on vacation, and you guys went out and used your own time to kill that thing, right? The money is yours. Buy whatever you want."

"Big Sister . . ."

"Okay."

Filo and I were thinking the same thing, and we both took

the money that Mr. Naofumi was offering us. Then I went for a walk. There were certain materials that Mr. Naofumi had wanted for his accessory-making. I bought them and gave them to him as a present.

"What is it? I said you could buy whatever you wanted. This must have been expensive."

"It's from both of us. We wanted to give you a present because you always take care of us."

"Yeah! It's a present for you, Master!"

It would have been easy enough to take it all . . . but Filo and I had earned it together, and we both really wanted the same thing. We just wanted to express our gratitude to Mr. Naofumi, and so we did.

"Oh . . . okay."

Mr. Naofumi smiled awkwardly and then reached out to kindly pat our heads.

"Raphtalia, Filo, thank you. I'll treasure it."

Ugh . . . There he was, treating me like a kid again.

The jerk . . . He'd never see me as a woman!

Right, Filo?

"Yup!"

We turned to face one another and nodded in agreement.

Character Design:
Filo (human form)

フィーロ (フィロリアル型)

Character Design:
Filo (bird form)

ツメ✕

フィーロ (クイーン型)

オルトクレイ

The Rising of the Shield Hero Vol. 2
© Aneko Yusagi 2013
First published by KADOKAWA in 2013 in Japan.
English translation rights arranged by One Peace Books
under the license from KADOKAWA CORPORATION, Japan

ISBN: 978-1-935548-78-2

Written by Aneko Yusagi
Character design by Minami Seira
English edition published by One Peace Books 2015

Printed in Canada

11 12 13 14 15 16 17 18 19 20

One Peace Books
43-32 22nd Street STE 204 Long Island City New York 11101
www.onepeacebooks.com